VENGEFUL SON

Andrew Allen Smith

To Gary and Laureen, whose undying passion and commitment to each other should be a reminder to us all on how we should be and whose constant encouragement began this quest.

The sun glinted off the water of the pool as Michael looked through the lens patiently. The slight flickering glare was soothing through the barely tinted lens as he scanned the home that was nearly 500 yards away. A brisk breeze wafted across the roof where he was comfortably situated, unknown to anyone, a ghost in the moment.

Michael shifted slightly to look at the side of the house. From this distance, a small shift allowed him to clearly see two distinct sides of the distant home. With the majestic pool in his view, surrounded by long grass, the scattering of well-placed lawn furniture, the nearly perfectly placed plants and the outdoor entertainment area that was so inviting, Michael considered getting similar in his less than modest home.

Michael changed the focus and peered into the large windows at the back of the home, his lens so precise that the simple change of focus allowed him to see inside as well as out. There he again saw the "Pottery Barn" perfect interior with stacked books that may or may not have been read and a 70-inch TV that seemed as thin as a sheet of paper.

If he had not been told someone was home, he would swear he was looking at a picture from Better Homes and Gardens hung precariously in front of his lens, instead of a house with several occupants and several secrets.

He adjusted his earpiece, listened and heard nothing. The small receiver in his ear was linked to a parabolic microphone he had mounted closer to the house earlier this week.

A sudden sound made him scan the house again. Michael saw the woman walk to the back door. He adjusted his lens slightly and zoomed in even closer. She was tall, he guessed between 5'8" and 5'10" by looking at the furniture and door frame. She was wearing long slacks with a black tank top covered by a simple white sweater cover up. She walked with a grace that could only be learned in a pristine boarding school or from parents who were patient and diligent at showing their child how important poise and manners were in the world. He considered his upbringing for a moment and how diligent his mother was at giving him similar poise, then shook off the thought as a distraction. He had work to do.

Michael continued watching as the woman came to a large set of French doors that led to the pool. She paused, looked at the beautiful area and her bright blue eyes looked down. Was that a tear? She kept her arms tightly crossed as though she were hugging some long distant lover who had been pulled to the wind until no more. Her hug became a hug to herself and now Michael truly saw her weep.

He was impassionate as he listened to her light sob, until he heard another voice. The man walked behind her. He was chiseled with powerful blue eyes as well and cold impassionate features. Outsiders may have thought he was handsome, but Michael knew his kind. He had dealt with so many like him before. Today it was not him he had to deal with.

He turned a small dial on his lens and the inner lights came online, superimposing a series of concentric circles on his view. His steady hand made those circles, even at this distance, as solid as crystal.

He heard the voice again.

"It won't be long now," the man said as Michael focused.

"What more can you do to me?" the woman responded, her long chestnut hair swinging as she turned. "You have left me alone in my own home, treated me as though I was not here. You have been dispassionate to me, but everyone thinks you and I are happy. I am alone in a marriage and now that my sons are gone, I have nothing but the pain of being with you, knowing I will never know anything but this."

"I understand" he said with a grimace, "but it is time for me to move on.

Our sons would never accept a divorce and you know I do not have any desire for you, so this is over."

Michael listened uninterestedly as he clicked one more click on the powerful lens. The tripod holding up his rifle and his steady hand kept the view still as he slowed his breath, clearing his mind. Michael didn't look at, but instead, looked into the woman. He could see her breath filling her lungs as she sobbed lightly. He could see her jugular pulsing slightly as her heart beat, her chest slowly rising and falling as she struggled to understand what her husband was saying. Then his target, Diana Fielding, looked up at the man before her.

"What have you done? Do I deserve this?" she asked.

"You heard our son. If we divorce, he is done with us. There is only one solution and it is not divorce. "

Michael saw his smirk again.

"I stayed here for our sons," she said. "I heard it as well. I stayed and I gave up."

The words echoed in Michael's ears. His scope was set, the 50-caliber bullet was loaded, his finger was on the trigger. Her heart was in the center of his scope. He saw the man's smirk to the side, he took a breath, slid the weapon a fraction to the right and fired. In his scope the man fell to the ground softly. The man he was not to kill, the man who had paid him to end his wife's life, the man who said his wife had cheated and worse. He saw him in a different light now and could not end her, but he had to make amends. As the man crumpled to the ground, he looked at the woman as she knelt to the ground and wept.

Chapter 1 – Passion

The sun shone wildly in the nook window as Michael calmly looked out upon the vibrant Appalachian Mountains. The sun was rising and the colors were almost pungent as another day began in pure light, giving promise to everyone who saw it. Michael watched the sun slowly continue to rise until it hit the hanging crystal on the massive back deck of his home. At the point the light hit it, the nook exploded with dancing colors from top to bottom.

It had been three years since Michael "missed" his shot. His handler was furious and caused him no end of trouble. Jobs had stopped and with it the money that gave him all the things he wanted. His weapons were his own and no one could take that from him. To get away from it all he had moved from his central Kentucky home to a home at the edge of the Appalachians on 700 acres he had been able to buy as a steal. His home was a testament to his life; powerful, quiet, yet strangely beautiful in a different sort of way.

With his parents long since dead, Michael had been self-sufficient for some time. His father had taught him very little of use except the ability to handle money and despite his now negative cash flow, Michael had a considerable amount of cash. He also wasn't really losing money, simply because his father had taught him a few tricks about dealing with stagnant funds as well.

Michael considered his predicament. He had no incoming cash flow except from his money born from the wisdom of his father, but if it wasn't for his father he would not be in this mess to begin with. An interesting consideration for sure, but the thought was frustrating to Michael. After he thought about it for a moment, he actually once again felt guilt and remorse and would have continued to do so if it hadn't been for Abby.

His live-in girlfriend was beautiful. Her long blonde hair cascaded down her near perfect frame. Where Michael was 6'2", she was a diminutive 5'4" and where Michael's handsome rugged looks and black hair made him look much older than he was, Abby looked to be only a few years over legal, if that. Their blue eyes locked and at that moment he set aside the painful feelings that were washing over him. Instead he felt warmth, love and passion. Those things his father had taught him to put aside, but his mother nurtured and brought back out in him. Abby wrapped her arms around his neck and as they looked at each other she simply said, "Hey, sweetie."

Michael smiled, his handsome white teeth glinting in the morning sun as he reached around Abby's waist and held her close. He liked being "sweetie" to someone. After all the things he had done it was amazing that anyone could call him "sweetie". He liked the feeling of love Abby gave him; he liked remembering life and love and passion and not the dispassionate, disingenuous parts of his childhood.

"Hey gorgeous," he returned and looked more deeply into her eyes. He was lost in the moment and he knelt down to her as his lips lightly brushed hers and she let out a slight moan. As she did he felt the electricity go through him, the electricity that he had felt his whole relationship with Abby. Time stood still as the kiss made his mind reel, as did hers as he kissed her, until they worked themselves into a fervor. He felt his heart racing against hers as the kiss became nearly uncontrollable. His hands found her hair and he brushed it back, then held her head and neck from behind. They slowed, as he looked back at her and slowly pulled away when she opened her eyes. She looked up at him with pure passion in her eyes.

"Wow," she said as he smiled at her.

"Wow is right," he said to her as his eyes seemed to sparkle.

"I love you," they said in unison as the doorbell rang behind them.

He didn't stop looking at her, nor did he even look towards the door. He was in the moment, he was in love, he knew what passion should be between two people and he had found it with Abby.

The doorbell rang again.

"You think you should get that?" Abby asked inquisitively.

"Do you think they can get in here?" Michael retorted.

"Well, no," Abby said, "but we have not had a guest in quite a while and it might be nice to know who found us out here, besides maybe a lonely elk."

"I suppose you are right," Michael said. "Maybe I should go check out who it is, but I really wanted more time with you."

"We will always have more time." Abby looked closely at him, "We should always have more time."

Michael smiled, but his smile was slightly empty as the thoughts from earlier came upon him again. He held Abby for a moment longer and hugged her forcefully, then walked to the door at the front of the house.

Chapter 2 – Compassion

The massive oak and steel door loomed before him like a silent sentinel protecting him and everything within his home. The sliding lock, two large bars that slid sideways and upwards sealing the entire frame of the door in four places, was mounted with a counterweight that he now twisted slightly and watched as the entire assembly moved diagonally, unlocking the door. Michael smiled a little, thinking about how secure this door truly was from intruders. It would take a tank to knock it down and by the time the tank got in, it may well be at risk.

The lock assembly reached its resting place and Michael unlocked the simple deadbolt, smiling again at the extra simplicity this added. He then turned the almost comically small knob and opened the door on its silent hinges.

Michael's look of shock was obviously visible as the beautiful woman came into view. Her long flowing brown hair wafted lightly in the wind as she looked at Michael with her piercing brown eyes.

Michael stood still, stunned as she looked in and said, "How are you Michael?"

"Madison?" Michael stammered.

She looked at him with a slight smirk.

"As if you would forget," Madison said dryly. "How long did we date? Four years? Five? I really didn't think you would have forgotten me that quickly."

Michael was still a little at a loss for words, which was rare for him. "Madison, how did you find me? Only a few people know where I am. What are you doing here? Does anyone else know you are here?"

"Nice opening. Do you think I could come in?"

A blonde head popped in under Michael's arm.

"Madison?" Abby said with a bit of a giggle in her voice. She slid under Michael and nearly ran him over and grabbed the woman in a bear hug. "Madison! It is so good to see you. We are so happy to have you up here." Abby was in her zone as Michael still stood a little stunned. "Out of the way Michael, Madison is coming in now. Are you staying long? How have things been? How are your parents?"

At the last question, Madison sagged slightly. Abby had dragged Madison into the large den while Michael closed the door and let the massive lock close itself.

"Something is wrong with your parents?" Abby asked quizzically, still controlling the moment. She moved Madison to the sitting area and a large leather couch. They sat down knee to knee next to a large cherry coffee table with a variety of steel sculptures ornately sitting on it.

Michael was at his wits end and looked at both women. He frowned and simply said, "Stop."

The two women looked at him. When he spoke in this familiar tone they both knew it was time to listen. Michael stood his ground in the center of the room, alone and away from the two women.

"Madison," Michael said in a controlled monotone, "how did you find me? What are you doing here? Does anyone else know you are here? Before we go any further, I need to know."

"Michael," Madison started, "No one knows where I am right now but the two of you. I found you by asking your mom's cousin. She didn't really give up much, but when I explained the situation she had pity on me and told me where you might be. As far as why I am here, I don't know where else to go."

Madison paused for a moment, tears welled up in her dark brown eyes. She swallowed once, then swallowed again choking back the emotion.

"Michael," Madison began, "Mom has been put in jail in North Korea."

She stopped and took a deep breath, regaining her composure. "You know she was always a free spirit, wanting to change the world with Dad, believing in anything she could if people listened. You know how she was. She and Dad went all over the world when they retired trying to make people see how life should be. When Dad died she didn't stop and she kept trying to preach to everyone anywhere and get her damn point across. The problem is that the North Koreans really don't care if she thinks she has a right and they are going to make an example of her."

She caught hold of herself again and was obviously flushed as Abby moved close to Michael and put her arms around him.

"Michael," she said emotionally, "Michael, they are going to kill her at the end of the month to set an example."

She paused, her perfect lips pouting in an almost cry. Looking at Michael she was pleading silently.

"What can I do about it? Call the government," Michael said dryly.

"I come up here and you say call the government?" Madison pleaded. "Don't you think I would have already called the government? Don't you think I would have tried anything before putting my sorry ass in front of you? Don't you see how much this is hurting me? Call the government?" Her voice quavered as Abby let Michael loose and moved to Madison.

"It will be okay," Abby said softly. "Calm down. It will be okay."

"Calm down?" Madison asked, "Calm down?? You know how Michael is and you know who he is. Who else could I turn to that could even possibly help my mother? Who else could at the very least give her peace and avoid this spectacle? Who else could possibly save her?"

"What makes you think I could help her anymore?" Michael said dryly. "I have been out and have stayed out."

Madison stood quickly and grabbed one of the steel sculptures in front of her and flung it at Michael's head. With a speed that belied his size, Michael reached out a hand and effortlessly grabbed the steel sculpture out of the air. He moved forward and set it back down in its place on the table.

"Any questions?" Madison smirked as Abby broke out laughing.

Chapter 3 – Condition

Michael turned and left the den with the two women still near the couch. He didn't say a word, which was again very rare for him. Michael opened the basement door and walked down the smooth spiral staircase to the large recreation room. He was upset, frustrated, concerned and feeling a little confused.

Confusion was not easy for Michael as he was always in control. Since he was little he had always asked "why" and pushed his mother for answers. Other children would conform or just do what they were told, but he had to push further. When told to do something he didn't want to do, he would open a debate. His mother, trying to raise a child that would think for himself, allowed the debate and he often won simply because he had the ability to see beyond the moment and look at the big picture even at that young age. He also found at an early age that he didn't have the burden of conscience that others did. His mother and father once admonished him for not listening. His response was to take his new knife from his birthday and carve just about everything into his expensive wooden dresser. When confronted with the damage by his parents he looked at them and simply said, "You told me to come upstairs and keep myself busy. You didn't give me guidance beyond that, so I kept myself busy." This earned Michael one of the few spankings he ever received in his life and it was a good one.

Michael considered his situation as he put on heavy bag gloves. Madison had come to him with a problem. The problem was her mother was a lunatic. When they were dating, Madison's mother hated Michael. In school, Madison was the liberal and Michael the realist. Michael went into applied engineering, but Madison could barely pull off her basic classes. Michael was always quiet and reserved, while Madison was overly outgoing. This had drawn him to her like a moth to a light bulb. It would eventually bring him and Abby together, simply because both girls were more like his mother than he was and obviously he still had some issues with his mother. His mother had loved both girls and they had both been to their house while he was in college. Madison was a girlfriend from high school and college, while Abby came along as Madison's college roommate's sister. Michael had often wondered how he and Madison lasted as long as they did with Madison's parents, Timothy and Karen Hiles, constantly berating Michael's more conservative views. Michael was spiritual. He didn't know what religion he was, but he knew there was something out there. Madison's parents said that religion was for ignorant people who were often blind followers. Michael loved weapons and was a champion javelin thrower and archer. He was one of the youngest consistent winners in trap skeet and target shooting in the country. Madison's parents didn't like guns and they didn't understand why anyone would be interested in them. They went as far as to say guns were for uneducated people. In the end, his conservative views clashed on almost every level with Madison's parents, but he had loved Madison dearly and she him. When Madison's father got sick during their Junior year, they pushed harder on Madison and she came to him one day saying she had to leave. At that time, she also broke up with him. She made her decision because of their wishes and it broke his heart. He had never let anyone close to him, never cared. His dad taught him that being dispassionate was a better way, but his mom had taught him love was more important than anything. He felt for a long time that his mother was the reason for his pain and in the end, it caused them their major issue.

Abby had been there one night to comfort him after Madison had left. Abby had been Madison's friend as well, but she was as frustrated by the situation as Michael was at the time. They went to a movie, then two, talked on the phone for hours upon end and became friends like most people will never know. When they went further, it was not just friendship; it was a natural progression from the passion they shared. Michael knew when he finally got to that point that his mother had always been right, but by then it was too late to tell her.

Michael started hitting the bag. Slow punches at first to the center of the bag. A slow jab, a slow hook, his punches continued building in strength as he started picking up speed.

Michael was lost in his inner monologue. Why her? Why Madison? Anyone but Madison. Why help her mother who caused him so much pain? He hit the bag faster, fast jabs with multiple rabbit punches after. Madison's mother, Karen, the pain in the ass. Madison's mother the bitch. She got herself into this mess because of her big mouth. He hit the bag even faster, an obvious sweat on his brow and his shirt began to moisten with the exertion. Damnit. Why did Abby have to be so nice to her? Abby knew how bad she had hurt him. Why did Debbie tell her anything? Debbie knew better; his mom's cousin often spoke before she thought. Madison was nothing to him anymore. His punches were now blurring as he hit the bag faster and faster. Damnit, damnit, damnit. The leather of the bag began cracking and split, spilling some cotton and sand to the floor as he heard a noise behind him.

"Michael!"

It was Abby.

Michael looked back at her, then grabbed a roll of duct tape sitting to the side of him on a pegboard.

"What?" Michael asked sullenly.

"You need to eat and we need to talk about Madison. I put her in the guest room," Abby continued.

"You put my ex-girlfriend that broke my heart in my house in the guest room?" Michael asked dryly as he taped up yet another hole in the well beaten heavy bag.

"No, I put your ex-girlfriend and my friend, and YOUR friend into the guestroom in OUR house and we need to talk about the whole situation," Abby said sternly. "And by the way, I really don't like your attitude right now. You need to get your cute little ass upstairs and eat with us before you pass out. Your 'mental condition' right now needs to be better so you can make a good decision on what will happen next."

Michael smiled, then laughed a little, turning around slightly showing Abby his butt. "This thing is cute?"

"Damn right. And it's mine, as well as half this house, no matter what you think. We may not be married, but this is forever buster. Your ex is here with a problem. We know you can help, we, that's right, WE, need to decide if you are going to help or if you are going to turn her out like she did you. I love you no matter what. Now get your ass upstairs, move it!" Abby said with that twinkle in her eye again.

"Wow," Michael actually said out loud as Abby ran up the stairs almost giggling. He was always amazed how she could take a sour mood of his and turn it into a positive one. It was something Madison could never do and only his mother had ever come close to the same. He chased after Abby up the spiral staircase with more than a little sweat pouring off of him and realized he was still holding the duct tape. Throwing it at the peg, he laughed as the tape rocketed across the room and spiraled around the peg three times, only to be back in its original resting place from over fifteen feet away.

Chapter 4 – Discussion

Abby crested the stairs and ran into the kitchen area being chased by Michael who was almost giddy now. Abby stopped at the counter and put her hands on the black granite countertop and Michael came up behind her and put his arms around her.

Michael kissed the nape of Abby's neck lightly and worked his way up the side. She shivered, then gasped as she actually had an orgasm from the kiss.

"Damnit," she said, "that is just not fair."

Michael held her tightly and moved up to her ear. "You will never know how much I love you," he said softly. "You will just never know. I will be here for you until the end of time."

Abby reached behind her neck and pulled him closer in a hug and he snuggled softly into her ear.

"Let me make you some breakfast," Abby said softly. "Want me to make something sweet or savory?"

Michael was again elated by this wonderful woman. "You are the sweetest thing in my life," he said softly.

She cooed as he kissed her neck again. "Now sit down and let me cook."

Michael moved to her side. "Let's cook together," he said. "It is always better when we cook together."

Abby slapped Michael on the thigh and got out a frying pan from next to his leg. "I am sure you mean breakfast," she giggled.

In his best innocent look he simply said, "Of course."

Abby and Michael worked together like a well-oiled machine. He got out eggs and bread while she fried bacon and sausage. With practiced ease he whipped the eggs with a little milk and began making French toast in a second skillet while Abby tended to the meat. She slipped out to the den area and the medium sized glass table overlooking the mountains and set the table with white placemats, napkins and silverware.

Sliding back to the kitchen Abby drained the grease from the meat, set it on paper towels to get out more grease and cut up three grapefruits. She put those in ornate little bowls and took them out to the table while Michael finished the French toast. The breakfast was cooked quickly and both Abby and Michael cleaned up as they went so there would be little work to do later.

They went out to the table and Abby went to the side wing to get Madison. Opening the door to the guest room Abby found Madison asleep on the king size bed. She went in and sat on the bed next to her old friend.

"Madison," Abby said softly. "Madison," Abby said again as she shook her lightly.

Madison's eyes opened and she jumped up. "I am so sorry," she said quickly. "I just have not relaxed in weeks."

"It's okay," Abby said. "Breakfast is ready."

"Breakfast?" Madison asked.

"Yes," Abby said. "It's that meal in the morning that makes your day start out right. Now come on out, we need to talk. There are decisions to make and it's early. We have a good routine."

"Yeah, how is that going?" Madison asked.

"Good," Abby returned. "He takes good care of himself and me. Honestly we could not be much happier."

"You really are good for him," Madison said, "Better than I ever could have been."

"Madison," Abby said somberly, "you know how badly you hurt Michael. Go easy on him. He still has a lot of scars. He hurt for a long time after you went back to your parents and it is a miracle he let me in. No one else will ever be close to him again. So, when you are talking, remember, he is who he is and you know about his mom. That just made it all worse."

Madison hung her head. "Yeah, I know," she said with a sigh in her voice. "Dumbest thing I ever did in my life." Madison took a deep breath. "Michael was always good to me. I am sorry to put you both through this, but I really don't know who else to talk to about the issue. I miss you Abby, but it hurts me too. Every time I think of my life I know I made a mistake and I know there is more out there. Michael found you. I was ruined. No one else was ever as good to me as he was and no one else ever made me feel safe. Do you know what I mean?"

"I sure do," Abby said. "I feel safe with Michael all the time. I didn't think I would for a while. You know, trust him with my heart. After his mom and dad though, he was a different man. More like his mom and not his dad. It just fell into place then. He had all the good traits of each of them and that made it worthwhile. With that in mind, Michael became something even more than either of them. He had his dad's good looks, his dad's money sense, his dad's dispassionate moods when he needed to, but suddenly he had his mom's passion for life, her laugh and now he needs to see more, to know more than ever before. He cuddles now; he hugs and truly feels more than ever. You remember his dad, Mister Disingenuous. He just was never passionate about anything but money. Remember how he treated Michael's mom? In church it was like they were not a couple, just two people on a pew. God, it was horrible. It is different with Michael though. Michael really cares now. My point is, and I am sorry I am rattling, is that you need to be careful with Michael. He still can be that bastard like his dad and neither of us need that."

A voice came from down the hall, "Would you two get out here before there are icicles on this food?"

"C'mon," Abby said. "We need to do this for you and your mom."

Madison grabbed Abby's arm as she started out the door. Abby turned and Madison said, "Abby, thank you for all of this. I am sorry."

"It's okay," Abby said. "Let's do this."

Chapter 5 – Decision

Abby and Madison walked into the den area and up to the table by the huge back windows overlooking the morning view of the Appalachian Mountains. Michael was standing, waiting for the two girls with a stoic look on his face as he said, "About time. Did you two have to go to the potty together?"

"You jerk," Abby said as Michael started laughing.

Madison really felt out of place with the two of them around. They were happy, even though they knew the somber reason she was here. It seemed unsettling to her, but also strangely comforting.

As Abby walked to the table, Michael pulled out the chair next to him for her, that allowed a beautiful view of the mountains. As she sat, he slowly pushed the chair in and she quickly said, "Thank you."

Madison on the other hand pulled out a chair across from the two of them and sat down on her own, even though Michael was still standing and moving towards her. She looked at him thoughtfully as she sat down, but in her mind, she felt that would be too much. She didn't deserve him to be nice to her. She considered the two of them, now sitting and felt she didn't deserve to be here and especially didn't deserve to disrupt their lives with her problems. It was her mother, but perhaps she should have pushed back on her mom more and stopped the irresponsible behavior that got her here.

Michael and Abby unfolded their napkins and put them on their laps, while Madison looked on. Madison realized it was time to eat and unfolded her napkin and placed it on her lap.

"This smells good," Madison said.

"Of course it does." Michael said with a smirk. "Abby is an amazing cook and she always treats me like a king."

Abby kicked Michael under the table as they started to eat. "He did half of this. Don't let him kid you."

Michael got serious, "So, Madison, tell me what you know about what has happened to your mom."

Madison set down her fork after only one bite.

"Well," she started, "Mom was in South Korea protesting the treatment of North Koreans in the marketplace. She was trying to do her usual spin on how the world should be free and what an unjust leader Kim Jong-Un was for his people. She had quite a few South Koreans pretty pumped. She spent a lot of time near the demilitarized zone and was really doing her same old thing, you know, pushing the limits. It gets weird from there. About twenty days ago she was suddenly gone and the North started sending pictures out to the South with her in them. She looked okay, if not a little harried, but they had her gagged and tied to a chair in all the propaganda. When I went to our State Department they said they could not really do anything since she crossed the line. I reached out to everyone I knew, including our senator. Mitch said he could do nothing. I even wrote to Dennis Rodman to see if he could do anything and have not heard back."

"So, pretty much a brick wall," Michael said at her pause. "Do you know where they are holding her?"

"Well, not really, but there is a view out the window that several people have been trying to enhance to see where it may be, but so far, nothing. It doesn't really matter. Mom has pissed off our country as much as any other, so I doubt anyone will go out on a limb for her. I keep trying Michael, but I am getting nowhere. I went to a mercenary I found through a guy working in the state, but they laughed at me and told me there are only a few people who could even have a chance at doing anything. They suggested I just buy some popcorn and wait for the movie."

Madison paused for a second as Michael took another bite of his French toast.

"I offered them $100,000 to get her out and they laughed at me."

Michael swallowed. "Must have been a smart merc to laugh. Doing this might be suicide.".

Abby kicked Michael again and he looked at her. "What?" he said. "You know it's not the friendliest place in the world." He looked back at Madison. "What then?"

"Well," she said, "they told me there was some guy in the mountains that might be able to pull it off. They said no one really knew where, but they had their ideas and I knew it was you. I avoided this Michael. Really, I did. I know I fucked up big time with you and you have no reason to care about my mother. I will give you the $100,000 just for letting me talk to you. I just do not know where to go. I even tried to talk to the North Korean government; they said if I gave them the $100,000 in person that they would let my mother go. When I told the mercenaries that, they said if I went they would take my money and kill me too."

"Yep," Michael said while chewing on a piece of bacon.

Abby kicked him again.

"You really need to stop doing that," Michael said. "I am getting kinda tired of it."

Abby smiled at him. "Then be nice."

Madison looked at them not knowing what was going on under the table. "Am I missing something?"

"Not really," Michael said. "Anything else?"

"I have all the files with everything I know in the room Abby put me in. I will get them for you," Madison stated quickly.

"No," Michael said. "Let's finish eating and I will see what I can find out.

I will look at your files later after I make a few calls."

Michael finished his breakfast and got up. Abby, who had not said much, just kicked Michael and stayed seated with Madison. Michael went to the kitchen, cleaned his plate and the few remaining items in the kitchen, then went back to the spiral stairwell to go downstairs with the girls staring after him.

"It will be okay, Madison," Abby said. "He would not be going down there if he had not already decided to help you."

Chapter 6 – Position

Michael entered the exercise room from the spiral staircase and walked to the back wall where various pieces of exercise equipment hung. On the wall were a series of dumbbells ranging from three pounds all the way to 100 pounds. Michael tipped the 100-pound dumbbell forward, then the forty, then the three-pound dumbbell and the wall clicked. He pressed the wall and it slid backwards on huge hinges that made no sound, even under the intense weight. Michael walked into the room behind the wall as white lights turned on and slowly glowed brighter as they came to life. Having entered, he closed the door behind him and heard the latch click again.

Before him was a 30 x 40-foot room with massive glass walls on both sides of him, along with a large desk at the far end of the room. On the desk stood six 40-inch monitors that were lighting up as he walked to them. He heard the massive fans of his computer spin up and slow as they gauged the temperature in the room and adjusted accordingly. His system already had a login prompt and he quickly entered the password. Instantly, all six monitors lit with camera angles around his home.

He focused on the central monitor and launched a program that would allow him to talk securely across the internet as he put on a comfortable headset. The headset glowed a soft green and he laughed as it was not really a com headset, but a gaming headset. He really could shred "Call of Duty" and did so from time to time. There just was no better headset for doing anything than the one he had purchased.

He pulled up his contact list and noticed he had several missed calls and messages on an older secure line. He pulled them up and listened. The first was a recording telling him his computer was calling their computer and he should call them to have them clean it up. He pressed delete. The second message was a little more interesting as it was his old handler.

"Michael," the message said, "I am hearing some clatter about an old girl you know trying to rent a person to take on something big. From what I hear this is hot on both sides. I am only calling you because you made me a lot of cash. Stay out Michael. This will not end well."

Michael pressed a key and the message was saved to a library of other messages. He wrote a little note on the comment tag, PARANOID GUY, and moved on to the last message.

"Michael," the computer voice stated, "for your safety stay out of it. I am watching."

Michael replayed the message twice. There was no voice easily identified. He ran it through a decoder and found it was pure computer synth. He tried to trace it backwards and to his computer, but it was as though the file were just created.

Michael clicked a few keys again and tagged the file, FOLLOW UP: FRIEND OR FOE?

At this point he clicked another key and brought up a dialing list and a dialing program. He clicked a small lock on the screen and a map came online, showing a set of lines crossing the globe. His computer bounced through a series of servers and ensured his call could not be traced. He then scrolled through the list of numbers until he stopped at PARANOID, then hit dial.

The number rang three times and then picked up. "Mainstream Travel" came the familiar voice.

"God, I could use a cruise," Michael said. "Maybe for two."

"Mikey?" The voice continued, "I knew you would be calling."

"Really?" Michael said.

"So, when did we talk last?" the voice asked.

"Well, it was about a month after you fired me," Michael continued, "and what did I say?"

"You said "deal with it" and I have," the voice said. "Good to know it is you. I hope you are not calling for why I think you are calling."

"You know I at least have to consider it." Michael said.

Michael looked at his screen and noticed one of the lines blink from green to red.

"Really?" Michael said. "Trying to trace?"

"Not me, Michael," the voice said. "This is too hot and it will come down hard from everywhere. Don't deal. In fact, ice the little twit and everyone will be happier. You may even get a seven-figure bill for it."

Another line turned red, then one orange. Michael knew he was being traced from multiple sources, so he would make this call tough and short.

"Same place," Michael said, "same time. Do not miss. I know I don't."

"Shit, Mike, don't get me into this." the voice said.

"Don't make me come see you," Michael returned.

He clicked a few keys and the lines on the screen started bouncing everywhere. In a few moments they started disappearing and then the screen was blank, except for a blinking cursor and a picture of Abby in the background.

"Fuck," he thought to himself.

Michael took a deep breath and saw movement on a monitor to his right. He quickly looked and saw a four-man team in black heading up the mountain towards his home and towards Abby.

Michael picked up the small phone to his side and pressed a button. "Abby, sweetie, could you collect Madison and come down here?"

He heard Abby laugh. "We are talking up here, you come up."

"Now, please." Michael said.

Abby suddenly got the point and Michael heard them heading for the stairs. He walked to the back wall and opened the overly heavy, but effortlessly movable door.

Michael then walked over to the drawer on the wall, opened it and took off his shirt and pants and began putting on a camo shirt and set of pants quickly. By the time the girls walked in the room he was fully dressed in camo and had put on a neoprene face mask that was camo as well.

Michael closed the drawer and left his clothes on the floor as he walked to the glass walls. He pressed a spot on the wall and the glass was suddenly backlit on both sides of the room with hundreds of weapons.

"Jesus," Madison said.

Michael slid his hands along a glowing spot and a case opened. He took out a small strange looking rifle with a long front and strange scope and a handgun with a large handle and long front cylinder.

"Really?" Abby said.

"Yes, really," Michael said, as he was pulling out two magazines for the rifle and two for the pistol. He put one of each in each pocket in his clothes designed to carry them, locked the others into place first on the handgun, then the rifle. He then slid the handgun into a holster on his right hip.

"What is going on?" Madison said shaking.

"Well," Michael said. "It appears you and Aunt Debbie have brought me some company. It is only fair I go out and greet them properly."

Michael touched a drawer to the side of a glass case and it opened smoothly, revealing a series of knives. He picked a large black knife that was marked "Gerber" and slid it into a sheath.

One more drawer and Michael got out a handful of zip ties, stuffing them into a pocket.

Michael opened his mask for a moment, reached down to Abby and kissed her softly. "Time to go play!" he said with a smile.

She looked at him. "They are not playing Michael, I want you back in here."

He looked at her and turned slightly, "For my cute little ass?"

She smiled a little, but said softly, "Be careful," as he walked out to the exercise room and the door closed.

Chapter 7 – Subjugation

Michael quickly lifted two fifty-pound weights on the rack, reversed them and watched the door settle to the ground. With over 1,200 pounds, he knew the girls were safe for now. He clicked a latch to his side and another door opened with a thin tunnel behind it. Michael climbed in with his P90, ducked and walked down the tube. After about thirty feet, he came to a large rock. He looked to the side and uncovered a small screen. Touching a button, it lit and scanned the area outside of the rock. Michael noted the coast as clear and slid the rock open, then closed it behind him.

In the house, the two girls were glued to the monitors. Madison was shaking like a leaf and Abby intently watched the men who were trying to be stealthy and climb the hill to the house. Abby was amazed as the cameras continued to lock on faces and movement and track the men who seemed quite good at being stealthy. They should not have worn black in the woods, but otherwise they were being really quiet and making their way to the house.

Abby knew the house with its massive stilts was nearly impossible to get into easily, except from the front. She also knew she would be moving, now that someone knew where they were living. She loved the house and would be sorry to move on, but Michael said they would have to someday. Besides, all she really needed was him.

Madison said, "Look," and Abby looked closely, noticing there were only three men left. The three had not yet realized that one of them was gone.

Outside, Michael zip tied the man in a hog tie fashion so he would not be able to get any leverage to even move. He had hit him with the butt of his knife and that was that, out cold. He knew as the numbers went down, the remaining would become more dangerous, so he needed to do this quickly.

Slipping to the side, he worked his way around another large outcropping of limestone and focused on the men again. They were about ten feet out and had not yet noticed their friend. He slid up silently behind them and as they rounded a large white pine tree, he took the last man. Grabbing him over the mouth with the knife to his temple, the man got the idea quickly and didn't struggle. Michael walked him back a few feet and put a sleeper on him. Moments later the man collapsed.

Michael carried him back to the area where the first man was hogtied and hogtied the second, first to himself, then locked their feet. Now, any attempt to move would cause pain to the other man and vice versa.

Michael looked up to where he knew a camera was and made a thumbs up sign, then jumped back into the brush.

In the house Madison looked at Abby and said, "Is he for real?"

Abby said, "More than you ever knew. He found in college he has a knack for complex tactics. Worked out better for him than engineering. Made me feel weird for a while, but I realized he was still the man I fell in love with. Even more so after his mother's death."

Down on the mountain Michael was working his way around again. The remaining two men were making much more noise than before as they had realized they had lost two. They were frantically trying to retrace and Michael moved to a clearing he knew they would come too momentarily.

When they emerged in the clearing, Michael simply said, "Stop".

They looked and began to reach for their weapons, but in a smooth motion Michael fired two shots from his FN Five-seven that shattered the handgrips in their side holsters without hurting either of them.

The men stopped and looked at him with disbelief.

"I really would rather not kill you," he said, "but it really won't matter much if I do. Knees please. Lock the ankles, hands on your head."

The men did so as Michael walked up to them, tied their hands with zip ties and pushed them forward. When they fell forward he tied their legs together, then sat the two back up.

"So, what should we talk about?" Michael said dryly looking at the two men. "And who do you work for?"

Chapter 8 – Inquisition

"You know who we work for," the leader said. "You have just attacked a representative of the United States of America."

Michael laughed, "You mean those representatives that invaded private property without a warrant, without cause and without a clue of who they are up against?"

"Oh, we know you, Jonathon Michael Masterson. We know all about you and your girl living up here. We know what you did in the past, for us and for others who could pay. We also know you are going to be taken in for questioning," the man spat.

"What you didn't say is 'How you will take me in for questioning?' and 'Why I let you live?' and 'How will your asses be saved'?", Michael laughed.

The man sat quietly. He looked around and struggled a little. Then looked at Michael and smiled, "Good questions."

"So," Michael said, "are we up for a discussion?"

"You know I can't tell you anything," the man started. "It would have been easier if you killed us. We have orders and you have a lot to lose, or so our orders say. So it would be best if you let us go or just kill us now. More will come and you know it. The girl led us right to you."

"Silly woman." Michael looked up at the camera, "I don't blame her, though. I blame where she got the information from. It does not matter. So, name, rank?"

"Alex Brown, Sergeant Alex Brown," Alex started, "assigned to spec ops just to find you. Is my team alive?"

"They will be sore when they get up, but they are okay," Michael laughed.

"Thanks for that," Brown started, then Michael moved quickly towards him and put his finger to his lips. Michael pulled his knife and in one swift motion cut the tie on Alex Brown's hands.

Michael ran to the front of the man, pointed two fingers to his eyes, then east. He then shaped his hands flat towards the south and moved silently into the brush.

Alex pulled a knife from his side and cut his second, Mark Sutherland, free. Mark had stayed quiet and quickly jumped up. Alex looked at him and pointed to the area Michael had just disappeared towards. Grabbing his M16, he crouched down and they began a slow cover formation towards the area they had last seen Michael.

In the house, Madison was frantic and Abby tense as they watched another group of four men head towards Michael and the small group he had captured. Michael had split off and again they could not see him in the cameras. Madison was simply shaking like a leaf and stammered, "What the hell? This isn't happening, this isn't happening," until Abby looked at her with a look that could have made lava go cold.

In the woods, Michael slipped to the edge of a thicket and brought up his rifle. The scope allowed him to quickly zoom in on the team in front of him. Unlike the other team, this group was "weapons hot". This meant that he had to act much more quickly and much more brutally.

He heard a snap to his rear and knew the US soldiers were moving up. All two of them. He should have left them tied up; they would throw off his timing.

Michael turned slowly to determine where they were, then turned back and noticed the four newcomers were heading towards that sound. It gave Michael an idea. He needed one or more of the new group alive to determine who the second player was, so he held fast and let both groups line up.

Michael knew Alex was trying to determine where he was, where the potential threat was and was trying to get the upper hand in the process. Michael didn't want his countryman dead, even though he could have easily killed him, so he waited patiently until the four newcomers crouched. Then with his P90 and silencer aimed carefully, he shot four quick shots that shattered four Steyr rifles. Michael then shot four more times and pierced the legs of the four men who fell, grabbing themselves in pain.

Alex and Mark moved into the clearing to see the four men on the ground moving towards the woods as they aimed their weapons at them and said "Stop".

The men stopped and put their hands up slowly. However, one man reached to his holster and pulled his sidearm, only to have it explode in his hand.

Michael emerged from the woods and looked at Alex. "Boy you guys are slow. You know he would have shot you. Hate to do this guys, but weapons down."

Alex looked at him, "Really?"

"Oh, don't tell me you have not thought about how you were going to take me too. Now weapons down. Let's find out who these people are and maybe you can leave in one piece," Michael said almost robotically. "I told you already, I would rather not kill you, but don't push me."

Alex and Mark laid their weapons down slowly and stood up. Michael threw a handful of zip ties to them and simply said, "Zip them up guys, it's time to find out who is behind the other curtain. I am sure these bozos followed you or Madison, but I am not sure who they are yet. I am betting North Koreans and not because they look like them, but because they are here and probably don't want me there. Make sense?"

As Michael talked, Mark and Alex tied the four men with zip ties and sat them up since the men were still struggling and shifting uncomfortably from gunshots to their legs.

"Okay guys, you want to watch or move back for a bit?" Michael said.

Mark was indignant, "We've seen anything you can do."

Michael smiled, "Okay", then rattled off a series of words in Mandarin, followed by Cantonese, then Japanese, then Korean. When he was speaking Korean, they looked up and one said something back to him.

"A good start," Michael said, "so how about English?"

"How about you fuck yourself," came the reply from one of the men in English.

Michael looked at that man, walked to him and knelt at his feet. "No thanks. And you should watch your mouth. There are ladies watching and this guy over here," he pointed at Mark, "I think he is still a virgin." Michael pulled a long zip tie from his pocket and looked at the man's leg. Grabbing it where he had just shot the man, he slipped the zip tie all the way through the hole and out the other side while the man screamed in pain. He then zipped the tie into a handle and lifted his leg up like a six pack.

The man howled in agony.

"You know, I really don't like to be mean." Michael started. "Well, sometimes I do." He looked up at the tree. "I wonder if I can hang you there for a while."

The man was sweating profusely.

"Now, wanna tell me who you are working for?" Michael said with a smirk.

"Kiss my ass," the man spit between his teeth.

Michael drew his weapon so fast it could barely be seen and shot the man in the other leg. As happened with his rifle, the 2275fps bullet wasn't hindered by flesh and bone and went straight through to the ground as the man began screaming again. Michael grabbed a second zip tie and pushed it through the new hole.

"Perfect," he said. "The boys who live in these hills love to hang deer in these woods from the trees." Michael grabbed a small belt around his waist and pulled it off. With quick practiced moves he unraveled the belt into a forty-foot para-cord rope. He threw this over a branch and tied it off, then slipped the end through the man's two zip tied loops on his wounded legs.

"Last chance," Michael said.

The man spat in Korean and the other three on the ground laughed, even in their pain. Michael quickly hoisted the man in the air as he shrieked loudly.

He looked at the other three who were staring at their compatriot with odd looks on their face. The agonizing screams kept going until Michael looked back and said, "Oops, forgot." Michael turned and in a swift motion slit the man's throat and sheathed his knife. The man struggled for only a second as blood sprayed. Then he was still.

Mark turned away and Alex said to him quietly, "Turn around and be a man. We need to know this as well."

"Good, now that the volume is down, how about English? Wanna tell me who sent you?" Michael said with a small grin on his face and a zip tie in his hand.

With an almost uncanny sense of timing, the hanging lifeless body fell as the zip ties and paracord had easily held the weight of the man, but the flesh of his leg had ripped until his body fell to the ground.

"Hate it when that happens," said Michael.

"North Korea," said one of the three remaining men with a defeated pale demeanor. "We are from North Korea."

Andrew Allen Smith

Chapter 9 – Redemption

Michael turned to the two soldiers and smiled. "See how easy that was?"

Alex looked at Michael with different eyes than earlier. Where before Michael was just another mission, now he realized just how lucky he was to be alive. Where most of the people he had dealt with in the past were predictable, Michael displayed a need to be in complete control. The files they had were woefully inaccurate as they only noted his previous accomplishments as an assassin, but they didn't outline the complexities of the man.

"Michael," Alex said, "we will take the other three back to our people and take care of the fourth, but you know they will come for you. You need to come in and deal with this."

Michael smiled, "You know I can't do that. You have been around at least a little. If I go in, I am done. I don't have the necessary leverage and for some reason someone does not want me involved in this issue. Worse, it is possible they do and are trying to force me in from a different level. If I go in, this does not end well any way you look at it."

Alex looked at the ground then back at him, "I have my orders."

Michael looked at him, "We are in a strange place then." Michael double checked the Koreans and looked back at Alex. "I should kill the rest of them and tie you up, to escape if you can, but I am considering letting you take them. To me this is a mistake. They will note how brutal I was and I will have yet another target on my back. I am trying to be left alone and if it wasn't for Madison, I would be enjoying life and doing as I expected, being alone."

"Of course, the other option is I could kill all of you," Michael continued. At this Mark and Alex looked at their weapons for only a moment. "I said I could, not I was going to. Please don't make me and let me finish." Alex relaxed a little.

Michael continued, "It would have been easier, but I don't think of you as evil. You are not a paid target and I am just wanting peace. My life has changed a lot in the last several years, but at the same time, I am not getting soft. I just want to make sure we both understand that."

Alex nodded, and said simply, "So where does that leave us?"

"Well," Michael continued, "I am going to go back to the house. I would suggest you get moving with the guys and get out of here. If you try to take me in any way, it will not be good. I am going to make a decision on what to do when I get enough information. This house is no longer a safe place for me, so it will be eliminated. I will be leaving with the girls. It would be good for you not to follow or report. I know that will be a bit of an issue, but you need to understand, I am giving you your lives here."

"I get it," Alex said. "We will give you the time you need."

Mark was silent most of the time. He finally opened up, "Are you really good enough to try what they say?"

Michael laughed. "I hope I don't find out. It is not a good idea either way. If I go, it will put me on the block. If I don't, it appears I am still on the block. Either way, I am in a bad place now because of someone else's bad decisions."

Alex looked thoughtful, "We see your point."

Michael looked around, "Time to leave for all of us. Your men are about fifty yards south. Get out of here. Things are going to get rough in about sixty minutes."

Alex put out his hand. Michael considered for only a second, then shook the outstretched hand solidly. "Good luck, Jonathon."

"Michael, please," Michael said. "Jonathon died with my mother."

"Another time," Mark said with a handshake.

"Under better circumstances maybe," Michael said. "I could take you shooting sometime," Michael grinned.

"Look forward to it," Mark grinned back.

Alex looked at Mark. "Get these three ready. I will go get the other two. We are out in ten." He looked back to Michael, but all that remained was the lightly swaying trees.

Chapter 10 – Evacuation

Michael swept up the mountain, checking occasionally for followers. As he came to the limestone edge, he found the rock he had come from just thirty minutes earlier. He reached to the side of it, touched a few spots and the rock slid open. Once inside the tunnel he sealed the entrance with the keypad and made his way back up to the exercise room.

Stopping for a moment, Michael grabbed a water from a small refrigerator and took a few sips, then reversed the weight on the wall and heard the counterweights allow the hidden door to move. Sliding the three weights again, he slid the door open to see Madison and Abby waiting for him.

Madison looked horribly shaken. She had the look of a woman who had been crying for a while and tried to cover it by blushing up her face too much. Abby ran to him and hugged him, nearly knocking the rifle out of his hands. Michael grabbed her and lifted her effortlessly as they kissed.

"You could have been killed," Abby said with a pout on her face.

"Ya think so?" Michael said with a smile.

"Not really, but I was worried," Abby said. "I think this has put Madison in shock. You were a bit over the top today."

"North Koreans are not to be messed with," Michael said. "If I had shown weakness at all, I never would have confirmed it was North Korea. We need to get upstairs and get out. Ten minutes and we will be gone from here. You need to get your bag of personal stuff ready and put it in the Suburban. Get Madison's stuff too. We will leave her car here. It will be here if she ever needs it, but I doubt it will be much of a loss."

"Michael," Abby started, "I really love this house."

"You will like the next one too," Michael hugged her hard.

"What is going on???" Madison almost screamed.

Abby looked at her. "Calm down," she said.

"Calm down?" Madison almost yelled "Calm down?!?!?! What the fuck? We just watched Michael capture four guys, shoot four more and kill a man. Fuck calming down? You must be fucking nuts to have him as a boyfriend. Are you as fucked up as he is? I knew his family. Michael has gone nuts and maybe you are too!"

Abby moved forward and slapped Madison across the face. Madison stopped short and was stunned.

Michael spoke. "Abby, it's okay." He looked to Madison. "Madison, did you think the people holding your mother would be nice people? They are willing to do anything to stop me since you got me involved and will not hesitate to kill you or Abby as well. You made a mess of this by coming here and bringing eight people with you. You should have let your mom die in peace. We both know she deserves it."

Madison looked hurt, but wide eyed as she continued to cry lightly and rubbed her face where Abby had struck her.

Michael continued. "Since we are going down this path, you need to get your head straight and realize this is not the fluffy sorority girl game world you think exists, but instead the real world where you kill or be killed and weakness is your end. Do you get it? Now go with Abby and get your ass in gear. We have to leave now. This house is compromised because of you and you can bet your sweet ass I will not be telling Aunt Debbie where I am next time."

Madison stood immobile and almost at the edge of shock. She resembled that person who has just found that aliens were real and was trying to digest it all. Abby grabbed her arm and led her out of the room and upstairs while Michael shut down his systems, grabbed some gear and headed to the garage.

Chapter 11 – Revision

Keith Smith and John Simpson were not in the best of moods. In the middle of Appalachia having just had their asses handed to them, they now had to deal with three North Koreans and a body while their target would be driving away any moment. Alex Brown and Mark Sutherland were busy moving the North Koreans down hills as Keith and John whined.

"He can't be all that," Keith started. "We can just bounce up there and hand him his ass and still be home in time for dinner."

"Yeah, "John continued, "I mean, there are four of us and we are ready for him now."

After just a few minutes, Alex had enough. "Three things, you morons: One, you just had your asses handed to you and you should be dead. If this guy had been any nicer to us, he would have put a blanket on you when he put both of you down. Two, if we tried anything I am now sure our intel is old and he has more eyes out here than a potato farmer in harvest season and three, I have the stripes. So, you need to shut up and carry the dead Korean that would have made your weak asses faint if you had seen him killed.

Mark smiled, laughed a second and pushed one of the North Koreans ahead of him as they made their way down the mountain.

Mark looked at Alex. "This will be one for the books, eh?"

Alex looked back at him, then their prisoners. "I doubt it is over yet and I am betting we will be in the middle of this in the near future. Don't get too comfortable. We just became the only two guys to have seen this man in years and lived to tell of it. Com will have a field day debriefing, then sending us out again. Look for promotions and travel in your near future."

Mark kept a close eye on his captives. "That is unless they find us to be the liability."

Alex considered for a moment, looked back at the two carrying the body, looked at Mark, then said, "I am hoping it doesn't go that way."

The four continued down the hill in silence, heading for the transports they had left on a road far below.

Chapter 12 – Explosion

Michael gave easy instruction. Get what you need and leave what we won't miss. He knew Abby would do the rest.

Michael went back to his special room, picked up a cell phone and put on a small headset. He dialed a number on the phone and waited for the voice. "Relocation," said the voice.

"Wheels up in three hours," Michael said.

"Cargo?" the voice returned.

"Suburban relocation," Michael stated dryly.

"Roger," said the voice, "proceed HTS, 180."

"Out," said Michael laughing to himself. He had known Jay his whole life and Jay knew who he was. He just always wanted to be more like he was when he was a Marine. Michael thought he could have just said pick me and my car up in three hours in Huntington, then a simple "okay" from Jay would have worked.

The black Suburban had more room than a family of six could easily fill, but Abby was trying. Michael had made three trips to his gun room and brought up the bare necessities. His FN Five-seven, P90 and 45 were the first in the car in a side compartment easily accessible to the driver. His Barrett and a variety of ARs were in large bags along with his Smith Model 41, a 22-caliber pistol that he just loved to shoot. In tins under the back floor he had four ammo cans of shells along with two shotguns and a variety of knives, explosives and items that only a ninja or a geek would know of or understand.

Abby, on the other hand, had pots, pans, assorted pretty trinkets and mementos as well as some clothes and Madison's small bags. Madison was still a nervous wreck from seeing the things Michael had done and still had a red cheek from her slap back into reality, but to her credit she had not stopped moving for the most part since Abby was the equivalent of a human cattle prod. Each time Madison would stop for a second Michael would hear Abby's voice yelling, "Go! Go! Go!" and then, stomping on the floor like an irate third grader, Madison would do as she was told.

Michael's job was easy. Like a nerd playing Tetris, he continued to maneuver items in the back so they hid his weapons and allowed the three of them to sit in the front two rows of seats without being beaten to death by a loose picture or worse, a rogue flower arrangement.

"Abby!" Michael yelled. "We are done here. Pick up the last of what you need and let's get moving!"

Madison came down the stairs with one more bag of clothing and with Abby, her blond hair barely out of place. Abby's drive for making things right had reminded him of his mother's intensity. "I think that is the last of it," Abby said.

Michael realized just how much intensity his mother had put into keeping him safe and alive. Her will to make life right for him had taught him much that he took for granted until his 21st birthday. It was then that he realized what a slob he had been, how entitled he had felt in his life and how poorly he had treated his mother. It was then that Madison had dumped him and his whole world began to spiral out of control.

"Thanks," Michael said. "I knew you would take care of me." He smiled at her, turned his back slightly towards her and continued. "You are always saving my cute little ass."

"It's my ass," she said slapping it, "and don't you forget it."

Michael laughed heartily and Abby laughed with him while Madison stood in mock disbelief once again.

Michael took the box from Madison, worked it into the back, closed up the Suburban and said, "You guys stay here. Time to go boom."

Michael went back into the house and ran up the stairs. On each of the

Lexan glass windows he put a small suction shaped blinking box. He did the same for the bedroom and kitchen areas. He then ran downstairs, lifted the weights and felt the massive door to his special room seal shut. He knew the reinforced room would survive and there was a second entrance to it under the floor if he ever needed anything that remained. On a wall next to the garage door was a small pad. He pushed a series of buttons and looked at his watch. It had been forty minutes since he left Alex and Mark. He set the timer for nineteen minutes, waited a few seconds and hit a key.

The timer started a relentless countdown to zero from 19:00.

Michael walked out to the garage where Abby and Madison waited and said, "Time to go. Hope you didn't have to go to the can or anything."

Abby got into the front and Madison got into the back seat as Michael got behind the wheel. He looked in the back seat where Madison was surrounded by empty space. "Abby, we could have packed more little flower arrangements; she doesn't take up much room. Oh well, too late." Then Michael smiled and winked at both Madison and Abby.

Abby hit him in the shoulder. "Jerk," she said, as the garage door opened and Michael drove out into the sunlit day. The day they were having breakfast just a few hours ago; the day that could have been so much better if he just hadn't answered the door; the day that started with a kiss that still made him smile, the kiss that turned into a fight he didn't really want.

He drove down the hill towards the highway as the clock ticked on his watch. As they slid past a holler (that is what they call those things in Appalachia), Michael got on the highway and headed towards Ashland KY, then Huntington, West Virginia across the river, where he knew a plane would be waiting for him.

As his clock got to one-minute, Michael pulled over and looked back at the mountain they had just driven from. He stepped out of the car, looked down at his watch for just a moment, then looked up. Abby and

Madison rolled down their windows and looked on as well.

"What?" said Madison.

Michael laughed as the clock finished its count as he saw the puff of smoke, then heard the explosion.

"What?" Michael said as he got back in the car. "The what is you just cost me a house. Oh crap, can I borrow your cell phone Madison?"

"Okay," Madison handed Michael the small smartphone. Michael snapped the phone in half and threw it out the window.

"Hey, that was mine!" Madison said in a slow whine.

"Sorry, don't want any followers this time," Michael said as Madison pouted.

 Madison again looked on to the smoke in the hills in disbelief as it rose in the early sky. Abby hugged Michael. Michael straightened and put the car into gear.

"We have a plane to catch," Michael said.

"A plane?" said Madison.

"Well," Michael said, "we sure can't drive where we need to go and make good time."

Michael pulled out onto the freeway and began the trip to Huntington.

Chapter 13 – Ignition

Alex 's crew saw the explosion from a safe distance as they were loading their prisoners into the back of their two vehicles. They cuffed the three men in the back seat of the first Humvee and put the fourth into the back of Alex's vehicle. Alex knew there would be no trace of Michael or the two women and was trying to figure out how to report this correctly. He also was pretty sure that the four men, or the three living men, would somehow get extradited to their country and all they knew so far was that was North Korea.

"Let's head to home, guys," Alex said as he got into the driver's seat of the lead Humvee and Mark got into the driver's seat of the second vehicle. As Alex worked his way into his seat, he picked up the headset for his satellite phone and called his commander.

"Sergeant Alex Brown reporting in," he said into the headset.

"Status?" came the voice.

"We have three suspected North Korean Nationals in custody. One deceased," Alex stated.

"And the target?" returned the voice.

"Target has evac'd," Alex stated.

"Unfortunate," the voice paused. "Sending coordinates for evac and two incomings will pick up near your location. Debrief on arrival."

"Destination?" Alex stated as calmly as he could.

"Need to know. Evac in twenty," came the voice, followed by a click as the phone was disconnected.

Alex got back out of the vehicle and went to the second. He tapped on the window and Mark slipped it open. "Take a walk," Alex said as he moved towards the woods.

Keith and John both got out of the passenger doors of the two vehicles to which Alex said, "Stand fast, we will evac in twenty. Guard the prisoners until we return."

Alex and Mark walked to the edge of the clearing and slightly into the woods. From here Alex could see the vehicles, but they could not easily see the two of them.

"Com is pissed or at least I think they are," Alex said quietly.

"Why?" Mark said.

"Just a feeling. They wanted this clean and now I am not sure they want any of it. We are set to evac from here and even that does not make sense. We could head north to Ashland or south a little to Pikeville and it would fit better," Alex continued. "They were just ... short."

Mark looked at his commanding officer. They had been in quite a few rough patches together and always managed to get out. "This is a weird one for sure and I am betting we have spooks in the middle of this. We have been okay before though, so don't worry too much."

"It's my job to worry ...," Alex retorted, "... plan and execute. This doesn't feel right at all."

"We will sort it out when we get to base," Mark said and turned to the vehicles.

Twin flashes hit almost simultaneously as missiles hit the two vehicles in the clearing, destroying them completely. Alex and Mark were thrown backwards into the trees by the eruption. The flames stayed bright as the explosion subsided, fueled by the two nearly full gas tanks.

Alex stood painfully. Looking down he saw he had a piece of glass in his arm. As he pulled it out he was thankful it didn't hit him anywhere else. The pain was intense and he considered he should be thankful Kevin and John would not have felt anything.

He looked over to Mark, face down on the ground. Kneeling, he turned

Mark over and saw that the side view mirror was embedded in his face with his eyes still open wide. Alex knelt down slowly and closed the man's eyes. Someone had answers and he had to find them.

Chapter 14 – Aviation

Michael pulled into the Huntington Tri-State Airport in the small gate for general aviation. He was ten minutes early and was ready to be done with the whole idea of driving for a while. Michael really enjoyed driving on open roads, but the roads between his ex-home and Huntington were a twisted mess of mountains, poor roads and unpredictable drivers, so he was a bit tired of it all. He would have preferred a BMW 750i on the long roads of the west any day or a nice convertible with Abby at his side on the California coastline.

Madison was asleep in the back seat and woke at the car stopping. "Are we there yet?" she said.

Abby and Michael laughed at the same time, then looked at each other and laughed again.

Madison said, "What?"

Abby looked back at Madison and just smiled, then said "Are we there yet, are we there yet?"

Madison groaned and rolled her eyes.

While Michael had a few minutes, he picked up the file Madison had brought and began skimming through it. There was not a lot of information, nor any real official statements. According to the file, the North Korean government wasn't taking credit for Madison's mother Karen, even though the videos sent out were supposedly from North Korea and promised a public execution. Also, there were no key players in the videos or in the files that aligned with any of the normal people involved in the political melee that was constantly North Korea.

That being said, it certainly seemed the US Government had verified it was them and the amount of information supporting the supposition of North Korea was high. The information seemed to be almost too good to be true, making Michael wonder how they had collected such detailed facts in a country that was often so secretive it almost ceased to exist at times. No matter who had her, Karen was in a world of hurt.

Michael closed the file and looked at the two girls. He simply said, "You ready?" as he began opening the car door.

It was then that Madison and Abby also heard the roar of massive engines and for a moment the horizon was blocked out as a massive plane touched down on the runway. The plane itself looked far too big to be on this runway, but somehow the pilot slowed the plane to a stop and taxied over to the area where Michael was parked. As the plane parked, everyone saw the massive, bagpipe playing, kilt wearing Scotsman on the front of the plane. The name "Happy Scotsman" was painted in large letters below the picture. The C130J Hercules was a plane used heavily by the military for transport and Jay McCloud used it well. His antics on getting stuff to the right place and right time were almost legend and the plane was part of that legend.

The plane's engines whined to a stop and the back of the plane opened and became a long ramp. From the ramp, a man who looked more like Santa Claus than a pilot walked down towards their car. Michael always wondered how Jay got his immense belly behind the wheel of the plane and how his long beard didn't get caught on anything, but noticed that his belly was much smaller than the last time he worked with him. Still, Jay always dressed with clothing far too loose, making him look like a homeless bear stuck in the woods that had been playing in a tent. Even with a little less weight, the effect was there. Michael stepped out of the suburban, walked to him and hugged him heartily.

"How's it going, Jay?" Michael said.

"Can't complain. Well I could; doc told me to lose weight, tired of working, wife is on my butt for a bigger house and I have more fun in this house than at the other one, but I love her, so I bring her with me," Jay said laughing. At that a cute middle-aged woman came down the ramp as well. "Michael, this is Janet."

Michael shook her hand, but in return she grabbed him and bear hugged him. "I have heard so much about you, boy," the woman said.

Michael looked at Jay to which he looked innocent and shook his head.

"Umm, thanks," Michael said, "but we really need to head out. It is a little hotter than I like."

"Good deal," Jay said. "Let's get this thing on the plane. Park dead center since you are it. Doesn't really affect much since this is nothing to carry, but under the wings is always better by the book."

Janet smiled as they began moving. "It always seems to be like this," she said with an impish grin.

"Back dead center, got it." Michael said as he got back in the Suburban. In this big truck he usually felt like the biggest thing on the road. As he started the truck and moved to the ramp of the plane, he now felt like the ant about to be swallowed by the anteater. Jay was guiding him as a garage mechanic would guide a patron into a garage, but this was much bigger than a normal garage. Madison's eyes were wide again as the plane seemed to swallow them whole until they grew accustomed to the dimmer interior lights. Once inside they truly felt as though they were in the belly of some immense animal.

Jay held up his hands for a stop and Michael was amazed at just how big this plane really was. As he and the girls opened the doors and stepped out they were again met by Jay, being jolly as ever as he latched the wheels of the truck down with cinches.

"Where to Michael?" Jay said.

"I will tell you once we get into the air and we should really do that right now," Michael returned.

"Okay," Jay laughed. "We will be up and running in a few. This airport is easy. Used to do touch and goes here a long time ago. There is a great bar at the Holiday Inn here."

Janet came down a set of stairs from the cockpit and yelled, "We ready?"

Jay yelled back up, "Coming right up. Let's get this show on the road," Jay turned to Michael and said, "You can come upstairs or wait in your car. It may be as comfortable. Once we are on auto I will wander down and let Janet sit on the controls and you can tell me where the hell we are going," Jay paused. "Ladies," Jay said as he tipped an imaginary hat.

The huge tail of the plane began to close behind Michael, Madison and Abby. Again, Madison looked like she was a cat in a bathtub slowly being filled with water. As the door closed and Michael heard the massive latches lock shut, Jay made his way to the stairs that seemed far too distant from the car.

Jay walked up the stairs as Michael, Madison and Abby got back in the diminutive Suburban. Moments later they heard massive engines roar and felt the plane begin to shake.

As Jay disappeared up the stairs, Michael got comfortable in the front seat and Abby moved the fold-up console to snuggle up into him.

Michael and Abby fell into a short nap while Madison sat in the back with wide eyes as she felt the plane take off and head to a location unknown.

Chapter 15 – Motivation

Alex was limping though the hills of Appalachia with his weapon and more questions than answers. Fortunately for him, the satellite phone was destroyed when they homed in on it with missiles to kill them. Mark should have survived, but now it was only Alex. Another truck was coming up behind him from a distance and Alex once again tried to wave it down.

This was the fifth truck that had come down this road in more than four hours and he expected this would be the fifth that passed him, but this time the beat up old blue Chevy pulled over to the side.

Alex put his M16 in the back of the truck and got in the front with the man who made Methuselah look like a spring chicken. His Coke bottle eyeglasses made Alex wonder if he would have been safer out on the road for a few more hours, but the man squinted slightly and said, "Where ya headed, boy?"

"Anywhere with a phone," Alex said.

"Well, I ain't got one and never seen the need fer one of them damn cell phone things, but I betcha there will be one up a piece towards Ivel," the man said.

"Ivel?" asked Alex.

"Y'aint from around here, huh?" The man continued, "It's a little town north of Pikeville. That's where you are now, kinda. You must be a revenuer to be out this way, ain't nothing out here but the big house on the hill and a bunch of poor ass rednecks like me. Gotta tell ya though, that guy up there did us good. He took care of my son and sent him off to college and told him to take care of his momma no matter what."

Alex considered how little they knew about Michael and how he was more involved in a lot of things the government had no idea about. "Yeah, I know him. He's a good guy."

"Yep," said the old man, "he is a saint, but damn ya better not cross him. Shit, I hear he can shoot a deer from a ways ya can't even see from and my cousin Bill said he came on him once in the woods and he drew so fast on him that Bill damn near peed himself."

"Yeah," said Alex, "I could see him doing that."

"Once my cousin Sue Ellen went up there to see if she could get him to go on a date, but she didn't know about the little blonde girl up there. She said they took her in and fed her, gave her some clothes and damned if she didn't just come back feeling like a princess."

Alex just nodded this time.

"So, I gotta ask, Mister," the old man said as he showed Alex the front of a 44 magnum, "you ain't here to mess with that boy, is ya?"

Alex sighed, "No sir. I was up here helping him and he had to leave. We got separated and now some revenuers killed my friends and left me for dead. Michael left so fast I can't get in touch with him and they have headed out. I will get in touch with him later, but I promise, we are not enemies."

The old man regarded him for a few moments as he drove, then swerved a little when he realized he was going off the road. As he righted himself, he slid the pistol back into a door holster on the driver's side of the car.

"I am trustin' ya," the old man said, "just cuz them damn revenuers are always in our business and you look like a good kid."

Alex sighed. He knew if the old man had pulled the trigger on the pistol at that range he would have been cut in half, but in the end, he was just too tired to fight it.

Alex set his head back for a moment and nodded off to sleep.

Chapter 16 – Division

Michael dreamed, it was more than a dream, it was a memory.

He was coming home from school early to surprise his dad. He was in his junior year of college and excited to go shooting, which was his passion. It was his birthday and he knew they would be waiting for him, but didn't expect him until tomorrow. He had skipped his last class just to be home to tell them how great it was going with Abby since Madison had left him. Sneaking in the house, he heard his mother and father in the kitchen arguing. He paused and listened.

"You're right," he heard his dad say. "I have never really loved you. It was fun for a while, but I am not attracted to you, don't love you and never will. I stay here every day so our son can grow up in a normal family, but don't expect me to give a damn about you. You should have been like my mother and just done what you were told. You have to be so in the middle of everything. Do you think I care about your friends or your family? Your job is simple; keep this house clean, do laundry and make money. You can't even get that right."

"If you are so sick of me, why stay?" he heard his mother cry.

"I am not going to be the reason for us to split up. That will be on you," his father said.

"Do you even care if Jon knows love or passion?" she asked.

"You stupid bitch. Passion is a waste of time and doesn't pay bills. I treat you just fine and I never have had to do anything passionate. Your stupid friends who are "passionate" about things are a waste of my time. You rubbed elbows with the bosses, now it is time for you to get real," his father seethed.

"Is Jon even important to you?" she sobbed.

"I wish I had never married you," his father continued dryly. "I should have left you and let you raise him alone, but something came over me

and I just couldn't. What a dumbass I have been to be with you the last twenty-two years. I really didn't like you while we were dating, but I married you so our baby would have a father, then Jon came along and I was really stuck. I should have left then. God, what was I thinking?"

"So just leave," she continued crying. "Leave me, leave us, I will be there for Jon."

"Nope," he said coldly, "you will not. I have him convinced you are the problem. I have led him to believe you are a liar treating me poorly. All the things you did for him and now you are going to lose him forever. He thinks I paid the bills for all his clothing, college, guns, bows and everything he has ever done while you worked your ass off for nothing. I have the money in the bank and Jon and I will leave. You will have nothing. I will make sure you have nothing because I have wasted my life on you."

Jon had heard enough. He stood and walked into the room. "Mom?" he said with tears in his eyes. She looked at him, her makeup smeared and her hair a mess. She had been crying and his dad stood above her, showing no emotion.

"Jon?" she said trying to wipe her crystal blue eyes. "Jon? What are you doing home?"

Jon looked at his dad and he knew the lies that had been handed to him. He remembered a few short years ago the two of them being close to divorce and his demand to his mother to fix it. He had told her she was a liar and he was done with her if they divorced. Now he knew why they were so close to splitting up then.

His father looked at him, "Jon, I..."

"Stop," Jon said for the first time to his father. His father moved towards him as his mother stood between the two. Time stood still as his father backhanded his mother. She fell in the kitchen and as she fell her head hit the marble cutting board next to them. Her head was gashed deeply

by the cold unyielding marble and as she continued her fall, the widening cut sprayed blood. The impact had done its work and she fell sideways to the dark kitchen floor with eyes wide open.

The bleeding stopped, but Jon's mother's eyes didn't close. As she fell to the ground and bounced, Jon's father realized what he had done. Jon rushed to her and cradled her slightly twitching body. Her blue eyes were glazed and no longer held the life that had guided him, protected him, empowered him and made him the person he was, without him understanding everything she did. Her blue eyes had watched over him his entire life, a life that now flashed before Jon's eyes with new understanding and a new attitude.

Samuel Jonathon Masterson reached for his son. "Jon", he said.

Jon glared at him coldly. "My name is Jonathon Michael Masterson. I was given my father's middle name and my mother's father's middle name to carry on our lineage, but there is no Jon anymore. I will never be Jon again. My name is Michael Masterson," he said as he teared up ever so slightly, then gained control. "I would rather be a bastard than be your son."

Michael reached down and closed his mother's eyes forever and as her blue eyes closed, so too did Michael's old views of the world and all within it.

Michael awoke with a start at his horrible memory as his ears popped and he knew they were passing 10,000 feet in the big C130J Hercules. He shook his head to clear the memory he tried so hard to forget each and every day.

The plane was livable, if not a little utilitarian. He reveled in the warmth of Abby next to him as he looked down at her sleeping peacefully. He didn't know if he deserved her at all for everything he had done in his life. He slid to the side and laid Abby down on the seat. She moved only slightly.

Stepping out of the Suburban, he walked across the deck to the stairs and made his way up to the flight deck. Once in the cockpit he saw Jay behind the controls of the jet still working his way up to 30,000 feet.

"Jay," Michael said, "head to Dubois, Wyoming. We will spend the night there. The airport will be a "fun" touchy landing and takeoff, but I have faith in you. Once we get the girls settled, we will need to head out. Janet will be safe there too. I will co-pilot."

Jay looked at him, "Michael," he said, "I know about this potential job. We can make a call, get help. I know someone."

"I am sure you do," Michael said, "but I am not yet sure I will do this. Some lines have been drawn and I need to erase them or end them."

Jay looked at him. "Heaven help them. I have seen that look before."

The plane banked and headed to Wyoming.

Chapter 17 – Salutations

Alex got out of the beat-up truck and sauntered over to the phone booth in front of a Dollar General store. It seemed there were always phone booths at Dollar General and the old man had dropped him with a wave and a smile telling him to "keep his britches clean."

Alex had change, but had not used a phone booth in years. As he picked up the phone and began dialing, he thought better of it, set the phone back in the cradle and walked to the Dollar General. He knew a landline could be traced in seconds with modern technology and he had to find a cell that could be discarded quickly, considering his last experience with talking to Com.

Inside the store, he went to the front desk and immediately saw a plethora of cheap cellular phones with cards for activation and service. He looked through the variety and found a simple flip phone design that would not have the advanced features and GPS of the more expensive smart phones.

Alex limped to the front of the store, still sore from his flight through the air from the focused missile attack earlier in the day and considered what a long day it had been. There had never been a day he had been deployed on a civilian pickup mission, had his team defeated so easily he wondered if any of them had training, saw a mark so poorly profiled, seen someone tortured in such an effective way and had teammates killed on purpose by friendly fire. Add to that where he was in rural Kentucky and he thought the day just could not get much worse. On the other hand, he knew that no other response team would be able to do any better than his.

He placed the cheap cell phone on the counter and the beautiful young girl with the fluffy hair asked if that was all.

"Yep," Alex said pulling out some cash.

"Ya know, my brother has an army outfit like that. He got it down at the surplus and thinks he is Rambo now," she smiled.

"Yeah, me too," Alex lied. "I just really think it's comfortable," he continued as he realized his M16 was still in the back of the old man's truck. He considered maybe the day could get worse.

"$32.50," the pretty girl stated as she got out a bag. "It should be charged. You get yours turned off? My brother got his turned off and he just buys a cheap one til he can pay the bill."

"Yep," Alex lied again. "It's been one of those months. Messed up at my job and it's just getting old."

"I know what you mean," she said with bright eyes. "They have an opening here, you know. You could start work immediately and they pay pretty good."

Alex smiled back as he paid in cash, "I will think about it. Thanks!"

As the young lady gave back the change, he took two pennies and dropped them in the "take a penny, leave a penny dish" and smiled at the young girl.

She laughed and said, "Thanks. There is always someone who needs it."

Alex walked outside and opened the small cell phone. He plugged in the battery and dialed the number on the card to activate the phone.

The metallic voice on the phone dryly told him he had sixty minutes of talk time. Alex dialed Lexington, Kentucky first to talk to an old friend in the city. After talking about a little of nothing for a few minutes, Jim Simpson simply asked, "Now that we have gotten the pleasantries out of the way, I know you didn't really call me to chat. What's up Alex?"

"I need a ride. No questions and no calls to anyone about me. There is a problem and the only one I know close who I can trust is you. If you can get me to Lexington, I will disappear," Alex said quickly.

"Where are you?" Jim asked.

"Ivel, Kentucky," Alex said.

"Ivel," Jim said, "People disappear in Ivel and never return. I think teeth do too, all the time." Jim chuckled and then laughed in the earpiece of the phone.

Alex groaned, "Don't make it worse than it is."

Jim laughed again. "I am on the way out the door. It is about two to three hours. Where should I meet you?"

"Looks like a Dairy Queen near the Dollar General," Alex said.

Jim started laughing again. "Okay," he said and hung up.

Alex considered calling Com again, but thought better of it. He was alone for now and it needed to be that way.

He moved to a stump on the side of the parking lot and sat down comfortably, looking at his surroundings. The mountains rose up to the sides of him and the people who lived in the area had found odd ways to live in space that most of America would run from. If anything, he had respect for the people here. They made do with little and made their lives rich and full. It was no wonder Michael had picked this area; the people were loyal, suspicious but friendly and welcoming to anyone. Michael could blend in easily.

Alex saw the truck pull up and beep hard. His ride had returned and he stood painfully and walked to the window of the truck. The old man leaned over a little and said, "Ya left yer rifle in the back boy. It's a good one, ya don't wanna lose it."

Alex reached into the back and pulled out the M16.

As he went back up to the front, the old man reached behind the seat and handed Alex a wad of cloth.

"Take this boy, I got plenty of them. It won't make people be so scared," the old man said.

Alex un-wadded the cloth and saw that it was actually a gun sock, which he pushed the rifle into, making it at least normal around these parts. As much of normal as it could be. "Thanks," Alex said.

"Keep it clean," said the old man as he drove off.

"Thanks again," Alex said and settled back down on his stump.

Chapter 18 – Deceleration

"I am landing this thing there even if you think it won't fit," Jay said over the radio as Michael looked on. "I know the risk and I can land in 5,000 feet, in spite of what the damn book says."

"You are not authorized to land at this strip. We don't have the…," the voice came over the headsets.

"Well here I come anyway," Jay said as he opened the flaps and guided the huge aircraft to the small runway. In truth, he had a few hundred or so feet more than the required distance for this plane, but he understood why they were nervous. After all, it wasn't like parking a Volkswagen, the plane took up space.

Michael picked up the headset and spoke quietly to the tower. "This is GYZa55 Heavy. I know you have concerns, but there is an expert pilot on board who I have personally landed with many times in this aircraft. Please let the controller know we will pay the proper fees for the plane once we are on the ground."

There was a pause, then a voice came on the com, "Land Runway One. Control will meet you at the hangars."

Jay laughed heartily. "As if they have a Runway Two at this place. This should call it Runway Two because it is a piece of shit."

"Cut them some slack," Michael said. "It's a small airport."

The engines wound down as Jay lined up the plane like a seamstress would thread a needle and slowed the plane to nearly a stall as he came down to the runway. Around them the mountains looked on in disbelief as the massive plane landed on a not so massive runway, but the outcome was never really in doubt. As the wheels hit the ground, Jay deftly reversed engines in a massive roar and slowly pressed on the brakes. The stop felt like being hung upside down and being spun around a pole as it pressed multiple G's on all of them. Michael was sorry he wasn't down in the car with Abby and hoped she and Madison were doing okay. Although Michael wasn't sitting down, his sinews flexed as he held on to the seats next to him to steady himself from moving. To a casual onlooker it would have appeared the forceful landing had no effect on him. The end of the runway was now in view, but Jay stopped short with over 600 feet to spare.

"Damn I'm good," Jay said.

"Damn you are," Janet said next to him.

Jay clicked on his radio, "Requesting gate info," then giggled.

A voice came back to him, "Park at the main hangar."

Jay moved the massive plane to the side of the terminal, the size of the plane looming larger than the terminal itself. He spun down the engines as a trio of men walked out to the plane. Janet hit a series of levers that opened the massive nose of the plane as Jay and Michael walked down from the cockpit to the cabin area.

"Think they'll be pissed?" Jay said.

Michael looked at him and laughed. "I think I need my wallet." He smiled and walked out into the fresh Wyoming air.

Chapter 19 – Irritation

Jim pulled up in a new Camaro a few hours later. Alex had been walking around, sitting on stumps and debating on who to call in the government to determine what was really going on.

As Jim pulled up, he rolled down the passenger window and yelled, "Need a lift?"

Alex limped slowly to the car and put the sock covered weapon in the back seat. He then carefully lowered himself into the seat and winced as the pain from his recent float across the trees nagged him in his joints and muscles. Although the makeshift bandage under his shirt didn't show, his sleeve was blood soaked and had turned a rusty brown as it dried in the cool air.

Jim looked at him and said, "Damn, you have a fight with your ex-wife again?"

"No," Alex said, "yours," and smiled a little. "God this has been a bad day."

Jim looked at Alex and simply said, "Happens."

The Camaro sped up the rural road and out of Ivel quickly. Alex looked over at Jim who should not have fit in the car. He was very large and very tall and his rugged Italian features made him look comical in the sports car, but Alex knew he was addicted to speed and adrenaline. Since Jim was 6'1", Alex was sure he had a hard time finding a big enough sports car.

As the Camaro passed eighty mph on the rural road Alex looked at Jim and said, "Umm, I could use not being caught by anyone in the government right now, okay?"

Jim laughed and tapped the dash, "Phantom, bet these hicks have never dealt with this type of jammer."

Alex looked at the weird looking radar detector and said, "Let's not find out."

"You are simply no fun Alex. You were not when we were in together and it hasn't gotten better since then, huh?" Jim said with mock seriousness. "I mean, WTF? You just take life too seriously. So who did you piss off this time?"

"You remember I always said everyone would piss off the wrong person some day and have their ass handed to them?" Jim nodded. Alex continued, "I pissed off the wrong person." He paused a moment then continued, "And got my ass handed to me and my team like I was an E1 just out of basic."

"Where's the team?" Jim said.

"Rather not say," Alex returned. "Probably said too much already. Really didn't want to involve you. But being stuck in Ivel was really not a thing I had ever imagined."

"You could have stolen a car," Jim said. "I know you remember how."

Alex smiled, "Yeah, but do you really want to steal a car from someone in Appalachia? I could have gotten blown in half by an old guy in a pickup today for just taking a ride. Imagine if I had taken a car."

Jim winced, "Yeah, I guess you are right. I still think if ISIS ever came to Kentucky they would just give up and go hide in a holler, afraid they might come over and visit them and kick all of their asses."

Alex laughed.

Jim kept moving up Route 23 as he candidly pressed the gas pedal and sped up again. He was tired of driving, but knew his friend needed him. As he went over a bridge he looked over to Alex who had fallen hard asleep.

Chapter 20 – Duplication

It didn't take long for Michael to solve the issue with the airport when they were informed he was the one from the hill. They were still quite amazed at Jay and his masterful flying to put the massive plane down on the small runway, but they were equally interested in the man who built the home in the hills that no one really knew much about.

Michael asked the small group from the airport to keep quiet about his appearance as he was a private person, but he knew they would not. People in small towns spread rumors faster than a cold in an overcrowded elementary school. Michael counted on some rumors getting started to keep him informed if anyone came just as he had in Appalachia, not that it kept Madison from getting to him. It had however kept some "revenuers" away in the past.

The loaded Suburban was now full as Jay and Janet shoved into the back seat with Madison. Where previously she was dwarfed by the big seats in the back, now Jay's massive frame and Janet's additional presence made it comfy, but not as spacious as it had been.

Michael pulled out onto the rural road and made his way down the small highway. After several turns and about forty minutes of being surrounded by mountains, they came upon a dirt road that seemed to head even higher into the foot hills.

The suburban didn't strain as it made its way up the twisty hill and came to a concrete pad before a large house. Abby blinked as she looked at the massive door that stood before them as Michael parked and got out of the car and stretched. As the others got out of the Suburban, Michael walked to the door. He tapped the door with his knuckles four times and looked back at Abby.

"Big door," he said.

She looked at him and was still a little confused.

Michael reached to the side of the door and pulled a panel open in the wood and typed in a short code.

Abby heard the familiar click and whir of the lock system she knew so well from her house in Appalachia. The door clicked and Michael turned the simple knob, pushing it open.

Abby shuffled quickly inside and coming around the bend of the foyer was greeted with the massive windows she was so familiar with, now overlooking the mountains of Wyoming.

She stood for a moment and looked back at Michael, then looked at the windows again as Jay, Janet and Madison walked into the room. Abby walked to Michael and hugged him. She peered around the room to find covered furniture set similar to the Appalachia house. Some dust was on different areas, but it was surprisingly clean.

"It's amazing," she said to Michael, holding him tight.

"Thought you might like it," Michael said as he reached down and kissed her softly.

Soon it would be twilight and the colors of the sky would open across their view in the panoramic windows. Abby assumed the windows caught the rising sun as Michael loved the sunrise and loved watching it come up with her each day.

"Jay," he said, "help me unload. Girls, unwrap the house. Abby, you should know where most things are. Why don't you set Madison, Jay and Janet up in rooms for the night?"

Jay joined him as they went out to the car and started bringing in bag after bag of clothing and setting them in the main room. As they went out to get more, the bags mysteriously disappeared. In her normal efficiency, Abby took them, which Michael thought would drive Janet and Madison not only to work, but perhaps drive them to drink as well.

When all the personal belongings were complete, Michael closed the truck and looked at Jay, "Let's do the rest the easy way."

Michael started the truck and drove around the drive to a large lower garage. He hit the garage opener and this garage opened slowly. Inside the spacious garage sat an identical black suburban and two empty spaces. As Michael drove in, the lights came on making the room easily seen from any point of view.

Michael got out of the Suburban, opened the back hatch and easily hefted one of the massive bags of weapons he had packed in earlier that day.

"We will bring all I brought in and I will decide what I need between what I have here and what I brought." Michael said as he raised two eyebrows with Groucho Marx flair.

He walked into the door of the garage and was in the den/exercise room where he then walked to the wall and lifted the 143 pounds of weight and heard the all too familiar click of the hidden door.

Michael walked into the room and the lights and computers came on, making him feel at home once again. This was his home now and in fact, anywhere was home as long as Abby was there.

Chapter 21 – Dissertation

Alex woke as Jim pulled onto I-64, heading west towards Lexington. He felt sore as hell, but a little clearer of mind. He almost smiled, until he remembered Mark and the issues of the day. It was sobering at best. Alex checked his arm; it was sore, but not as much as it could have been.

"Nice nap," Jim said as he sped up.

"Thanks," said Alex as he shook his head a little. "I think I need to make a call. Can you pull over for a moment? If the call goes south, we will need to be gone quickly."

"Oh, one of those calls," Jim said solemnly. "I took the faster way for me and got to US60 before we hit I-64. There is a rest area in a few moments as we pass Mount Sterling."

As if on cue, the blue Rest Area sign showed up in the headlights and Alex smiled. Jim knew directions and roads like most people knew their home floorplans.

"That's good," Alex said, as the road flashed before them and in less than a minute they were pulling off to the rest area.

Jim said, "Bathroom break," and walked to the building while Alex walked to an area off to the side of the road where he would not be heard.

Alex dialed the call-in number on his little cheap phone and waited. After three rings the phone answered.

"Sergeant Alex Brown reporting in," Alex said.

A female voice this time stated, "Transferring..."

A few seconds passed and suddenly he heard a new voice. "What the fuck is going on with you? I had you reported dead and your Com has disappeared."

"Sam?" Alex said in a questioning tone.

"That would be General Sam to you or Sir, General Sir," came the voice.

"Sorry sir, is the channel secure?" Alex stated.

"No the fucking channel is not secure. You are on a fucking cell phone. Is there some type of landline where you are we can secure?" the general asked.

"I am not sure. Request secondary call in one hour," Alex said.

"You better fucking get your ass in here after that call. There is a lot of shit that was piled on my desk this morning, including your tags. You don't sound tagged though, so I will give you one hour to get secure, call me and start lighting up my day instead of shitting on it like your Com has done," the general barked.

"Sir, yes sir," Alex said quickly. "One hour."

Alex flipped the phone off and took out the battery. He may need it again, but removing the battery eliminated the chance of anyone finding him through the phone.

Jim was back to the car.

"How did it go?" Jim said.

"Strange," Alex returned. "I am not sure who or what to believe at the moment. Can you get me to a secure line in Lexington in one hour from here?"

"You mean I can speed?" Jim said with childish mischief in his voice. "You are damn straight. I will have you there!"

It wasn't really that far from Mount Sterling to Lexington, but Alex needed a secure line and that would take a few minutes to find. It was hard to find anyone with a landline anymore. He could grab a smartphone and use that, but a landline seemed to make sense and he could be gone at any moment with Jim around.

"Any ideas on the line?" Alex said to Jim.

"Sure," Jim said. "Plenty of choices in the Hamburg shopping area. Piece of cake and we can be gone in seconds if we need to be. Damn this is fun."

Alex thought for a moment; this wasn't really his idea of fun. He watched the road pass before him like a "light speed" animation and wondered how fast Jim would have to drive to outrun a missile. Alex shuddered at the thought and hoped he never had to find out.

Chapter 22 – Deletion

Michael sat in front of the now humming computer while Jay brought in the second heavy bag of weapons.

"What else is in the truck?" Jay asked as he sat the bags on the floor next to the two Michael had bought in.

"Four ammo cans under the back seats, that should be all," Michael answered. "Then come sit with me for a second so we can figure this out."

"On it," Jay huffed as his huge body lumbered back out through the door.

Michael was doing simple internet searches for Karen Hiles to determine any possible information that could be public at this time.

Search after search brought up lots of information about Karen and her liberal opinions. Different searches brought up tons of information about her activism, a few articles about Tommy, her now deceased husband, and even fewer about their daughter Madison. It was the last piece that piqued Michael's attention for a moment. One of the pictures of Karen and Madison contained Michael.

Michael thought he had removed all pictures from the internet that could associate anyone with him, years before. When Michael was recruited for his unique abilities, Madison was still in the picture and he was still in college. A brief trip to Rome during his junior year would allow him to eliminate an issue, then he would swing back to school with no negative thoughts about what he had done. During that time, he was as unfeeling about everything in life as his father had been.

Madison had begun asking questions and since he thought he had loved her, he had given her some information. Perhaps too much, he thought to himself as Madison was a little odd about the whole thing. As he considered what he had told her, he almost laughed to himself. How do you tell your girlfriend you make money and paid off your school loans the first job you did by killing an Arab terrorist overseas to the tune of $500,000?

Because of her response, Michael had stayed a little quiet about it. Could she have told her mother? Is that why she was targeted? Was it to get to him? He had a lot of questions, with no answers. He needed to find answers with Madison.

He was still thinking about it all when Jay dropped the ammo cans on the floor behind him.

"Damn," Jay said, "These things are heavy. I have never known you to use more than one bullet on a job. Why so many?"

"It was just to wear you out so I could sleep tonight," Michael laughed.

"It worked," Jay said. "Did you really need me or can I go check on the girls?"

"Go ahead and check," Michael said in a distracted tone. "We will go through everything before we leave in the morning. I will be a little bit. Let Abby know I will be up soon."

"Gotcha," Jay said as he looked at the screen. "Old stuff huh, you were young there. 'Bout the time I first met you, isn't it?"

"Around there," Michael noted. "I will be up soon."

"Gotcha," Jay grinned. "I will be up soon means 'stop annoying me and go away'. I get it now."

Michael smiled, "Yep."

Jay turned and walked to the door. "Goodnight," he said and disappeared from Michael's view.

Michael kept looking, but found no additional photos or connections to him and Madison. He set a program to wipe out the one he had just found. The program would worm its way through servers looking for references to the files and delete them as possible. It would take a lot of time, but it was effective as it listened to network traffic, built decryption keys and eventually found a way in. Michael had not written it, but he had been given the 'bot' by a grateful customer a long time ago and occasionally received an update.

Where the picture had hurt like an old sports injury, he now thought of the aftermath and of Abby and how she had turned his life around. She had been there when Madison had devastated him and had accepted everything about him. Where Madison had issues with what he had begun doing, Abby was just there for him and loved who he was in spite of what he was going through. In the beginning he was more aloof with her, but after his mother, he saw her as the most special woman in the world and treated her not only as an equal, but with a respect that would have made his mother proud. He only wished his mother had lived to see him stop being the selfish ass he had been before, the one who had no care for anyone but himself.

He sighed and continued his searches until he heard a noise from behind. He turned and there was Abby. She was wearing a long black silken kimono and her blond hair draped over the black silk creating a contrast more prominent that the yin-yang symbol of the east.

She walked to him. "The others are in bed or going to sleep soon. It has been a long day Michael. Come be with me."

He was as mesmerized by her beauty as he always was and felt flushed and excited.

Abby reached him. As she put her arms around him, her kimono opened and her perfect skin and breasts surrounded Michael's head. Michael sat in his chair and kissed her skin, working up to the tender skin between her breasts. She moaned and Michael stood, lifting her effortlessly.

Abby slowly slid down his arms until they were standing face to face. He kissed her, hard and passionately, like it was their first and last kiss. She returned the kiss even more forcefully, then pulled back.

"Let's go upstairs," she said.

"Agreed," Michael said as they went to the door together.

Behind Michael on the screen the voicemail icon blinked silently as the huge door snapped shut.

Chapter 23 – Aggravation

Alex was annoyed.

In the last thirty years, phone booths had gone from being a staple across the world, to being a rarity, except in television shows where they were actually massive inside and flew around the universe or parts of dumb gags for Superman and other movies. In a world with cell phones, few people actually realized the depth of privacy they were giving away as a cell phone could be monitored, tracked and hacked, allowing much more information to be gathered than what people should want public.

After running in circles for a short time, Alex and Jim found a convenience store with a phone booth and after using a rag to clean the unidentifiable substance that would make a Billy goat gag from the handset, Alex dialed the secure number to Com.

After three rings the phone answered. "Sergeant Alex Brown reporting in."

A female voice returned, "Transferring..."

The female voice came back online, "Securing line."

A gruff voice bellowed, "About damn time. Do you have any idea what time it is? My ass should not be babysitting this late."

"Yes, sir," Alex stated. "Reporting via secure line, as requested."

"Yeah, yeah," the general continued, "fill in the blanks. What the fuck happened this morning?"

Alex started in a skilled monotone. "This morning we were given orders to obtain and detain Jonathon Michael Masterson. We were not given solid intel and were under the impression his status was currently non-combative. Masterson subdued the team rapidly and with no apparent effort, at the conclusion of which myself and Sutherland were released. Masterson engaged and subdued four hostiles whom he interrogated and identified as North Korean. It was apparent we were used as a distraction to give him an advantage in subduing the hostiles. Masterson then released us and apparently blew up his own home to cover his tracks. His whereabouts are unknown. Upon reaching our transport and calling into Com, we were told to wait for pickup. Sutherland and I were in tree cover when missiles destroyed our transport and debris killed Sutherland. I have been rogue since."

The general cleared his throat and started, "Well boy, this sure is a mess. This does not match our report, which is a pooch screw to say the least, and we have no good reason for you to be there to begin with. I will have to look into this shit to figure out what the fuck was going on. Masterson is not a designated target officially and knowing him and who I know keeps eyes on him, we should have been a little more candid with any type of assault or meet and greet or whatever the fuck you thought you were doing. I am surprised the little fuck didn't kill you for fun, but I had heard he has softened up a bit and gone off grid. Why the fuck we would want him back on grid is beyond me. Little shit like that might just as well stay in his hole and I would be happier. As it is, his very existence chaps my ass every day I look at my wall."

"Yes sir," Alex stated.

"Now listen up," the general continued ignoring Alex completely. "You need to get your ass to Bluegrass Army Depot. They will not know what to do with you, but I will have someone there. No bullshit, no detours. Get your ass there now and we will fly you to a secure location tomorrow."

Alex didn't reply immediately.

"Alex, I know we have history, but this is a bunch of shit and you need to suck it up and at least trust me. There are things going on here that neither of us knows. That damn spook you talked to this morning has gone AWOL and I have no direct orders except to find out what the fuck is going on and who the fuck is messing with my people. Get me?" the general spat.

"Yes sir. I will get there ASAP," Alex stated.

"You do that and don't doddle around for cheeseburgers or tits. Just get your ass to base," the general said and the line went dead.

Alex hung up the phone and got in the car.

Jim looked at him, "Fixed?"

"Nope. Can you get me to the Army Depot?" Alex questioned.

"Sure, why not?" Jim said and revved the engine before putting it into gear. This was his city and as any normal eighteen-year-old would do, Jim screeched the tires as he drove off. Problem was, Jim was a lot older than eighteen.

Chapter 24 – Expectations

Abby's naked body was tucked into Michael's arms as they spooned. She had fallen asleep quickly and was lightly snoring or "purring", as he liked to call it. He brushed her hair and she stirred unconsciously and pushed into him. He felt the most content feelings of his life with Abby. He wished he could have shared that with someone, but he had no family left except a crazy aunt and a few cousins. Abby's body was the perfect fit for him in every way and her mind was so in tune with Michael they could finish each other's sentences. Abby loved to talk and Michael would just listen. Several times she would say "Are you there?" or "Am I talking too much?" and he would just say, "I love the sound of your voice." And he did. He had talked to her on the phone all the time and listened to her at home all the time. Once she had stated, "I just don't deserve you. You listen and do everything for me and I don't do the same for you." Michael had looked her deep in the eyes and simply said, "You are everything I have ever wanted in my life and I never knew it. You deserve everything I can give you and more." Another time she said, "I feel like I am in your way," to which Michael replied seriously, "you are never in my way, you are my way."

Michael wondered if his mother had ever felt that close to anyone, ever, and dismissed the thought since he knew just how miserable she was all the time with his father. He had not seen it until that awful night, but realized his mother had lived a lie so well, his mind could not tell. Other people had no inkling, even now.

Michael brushed his hands across Abby's arm and kissed her shoulder lightly. She cooed in her sleep and he smiled. Even asleep they knew each other's touch so well. Michael's eyes slowly became heavy and he fell into a deep sleep.

Michael dreamed.

He held his mother's lifeless body in his arms and for the first time in a very long time, he cried.

He looked up at his father's panicked looks an yelled, "Call the ambulance and the police, you idiot."

His father grabbed the phone and dialed and in moments the ambulance was there. As the police filed in, Michael was still crying. He looked to them, then his father.

"He killed her. He hit her and she fell and now she is dead," Michael said in his still sobbing voice.

His father looked on and said quietly, "It was an accident."

The emergency medical technicians ushered Michael aside as they tried to revive her, but Michael knew it was too late.

Michael looked at his father, shook his head and looked at the police. "Arrest him, please. I got here in time to hear them argue. He was being aggressive and when she tried to defend herself, he hit her and killed her."

"She deserved what she got, but I didn't mean to kill her. You know that, Jon," Michael's dad stated.

"I know you just admitted you killed her, in front of six witnesses. And my name is Michael," Michael said dryly as the tears disappeared from his face.

"It was you who deserved to be gone. You who should be no more. She loved life and you love nothing. I may have caused her to stay with you, but I was wrong and now it appears I was dead wrong," Michael said solemnly.

The police read his father his rights as he begged Michael for forgiveness. "What can I do?" his father pleaded.

"You could have shown my mother happiness. You could have protected

her and protected how she felt. Instead you put her in her grave. Now you can't do anything."

Michael stood and waited and his dream changed as the police left, as the EMTs left. He was alone in the massive house. He was alone with nothing but his thoughts.

Everything he had thought was true in the world was being shaken to the core. All the things his father had taught him were in question. He had money now, as he had been "busy for over a year". Now he needed to clean some things up.

The dream shifted and he was with his rifle, the scope pointed some distance away. The trial was over; justice was not served: Innocent. Michael had been there, there was no innocence. Michael looked through the rifle's scope, focused on the target. This would be the last time he saw his father's face. The cross hairs lined up; he felt no remorse, no pity, no feeling except the longing for a different life. He squeezed the trigger, heard the shot and looked away knowing his father had fallen to the ground, knowing he was done being Jonathon forevermore.

Michael woke in a hot sweat. He was next to Abby still in the dark of night. His heart was beating fast, but he took a deep breath and felt his body calm under his control. He slowed, hugged Abby close to him and then fell back to a dreamless sleep.

Chapter 25 – Station

Jim pulled up in front of the Army Depot and looked at the gates.

"Ick," Jim said, "I really don't wanna be here. I forgot I am allergic to these places now."

"Just drop me at the gate…" Alex said in a monotone, "…you baby."

Jim laughed and they pulled to the main gate. The guard leaned down "Yes sir?" he said.

"Sergeant Alex Sutherland," Alex said as he leaned over towards Jim.

"Hold one moment, sir," the guard said as he turned and spoke into a phone he had taken from the wall.

The guard turned to them and looked to Alex, "ID please, sir."

Alex pulled a small bi-fold ID card from his shirt jacket pocket and handed it past Jim to the guard.

The guard stepped back to the phone, said a few words into the phone then came back to the car. Looking at Jim he said, "Your ID, sir."

"I'm just the ride," Jim said.

"Your ID, sir," said the guard in a slightly more serious tone.

Jim looked at Alex and said, "Damn you for getting me into this," and pulled his wallet from his back pocket. He handed his driver's license and retired military ID.

The guard spoke into the phone, nodded a few times and turned back to the Camaro. Handing all of the IDs back to Jim he said, "Proceed through and veer left, then follow the road until you are received."

Jim handed Alex's ID to him and laughed, "Fricken me in a base again. Crap."

As the gate opened Jim floored the car and laid about a foot of rubber on the ground, then slowed and laughed.

Alex looked at him, "You are going to get us shot."

"Surprised we are not dead yet anyway," Jim laughed, "but somebody wants you if we made it this far."

"...and you too," Alex said, "or I would be going alone now."

"That ain't good," Jim laughed as he made the left and worked his way up the road. As he pulled up the main road the car was met by a small platoon of soldiers. The lead held up her hand in an obvious motion meant to compel a stop.

"Nope, not good at all," Jim whistled.

A loud female voice stated, "Please step out of the car."

"Damnit," Jim said. "They might hurt my car."

"Shut up," Alex said as they both got out of the car with arms slightly raised.

The lead came up, a pretty young woman who was taller than Alex and literally bristled with muscles. As she came closer she was even more intimidating, standing at least 6'3" and rock solid. "Corporal Rachel Brown, sir. I am to be your guard until the general arrives. We don't get many visitors here sir. We have been informed the general is on his way and we will achieve our goal."

Rachel turned to the group behind her. "Smithers, stow the car. You two," she pointed to the two front men, "get inside and get them beds for the night. I want guards up all night in rotation."

Alex and Jim looked at each other as Rachel turned and said, "Follow me, sirs."

"Work out much?" said Jim as he hurried to keep up.

"Yes, sir," Rachel said. "At least twice a day."

"Date?" Jim smiled.

She looked down at him, "C'mon tiny, stick with women your own size."

"You are a woman my size," Jim laughed. "Perfect. I have never gone out with someone taller than me. How tall are you, corporal?"

"Six foot four inches," she said in a mock monotone, "a bit taller than you, tiny."

"Nice," Jim said as they walked into the brightly lit bunker.

Alex lagged behind and wondered. Wondered how this super long day would end. Was it over now or was there more to come? Where had Michael gone? What was the endgame in all of this and how he was going to inform the families of his team what had happened? The last he thought he should do pretty quickly. He was tired. Very tired, even after his hour-long nap in the car.

As they rounded a short hall there were two men waiting for them in front of a door. They opened the door as Rachel approached. "This will be yours for the night. There will be guards inside and out, you will have full freedom, but we were told you are to be protected no matter what, so don't mess with me or my guards."

Jim laughed again, "What if I want to mess with you?"

Rachel looked at Jim. "Sir, you would not last round one with me. I need a little more of a man to get my blood flowing, but if you want to meet in the gym, I spar at 0500 every morning and I am sure someone will give up their spot for you."

"Ohh, kinky," Jim laughed.

Rachel rolled her eyes and continued in her official tone, "Mess at 0600, the team will escort you. I have been told the general is in route and will be here about 0730. Sleep fast."

Alex walked into the room and looked at the six bunks. He took the one closest to a defensible wall. Sat down on the bunk, took off his boots, took off his jacket and fell asleep on top of the covers.

Jim looked on, took a further bunk and laid down thinking about how a ride had turned into an adventure. He looked at his watch and saw it was after 1AM. Looking up, he smiled to himself and thought he should get up and see just how good Rachel was, but snickered as he considered how much pain that could cause him or her on such little sleep. He stared up at the ceiling and he too drifted off to sleep.

Chapter 26 – Intimidation

Jim woke at 4:30AM with a start. Alex was still asleep and Jim wondered just how bad his day had been. In spite of his short sleep he decided quickly that it would be fun to see just how out of practice he was and get some jabs in on Rachel.

He walked to the door and opened it to the hall as two young guards jumped up to attention to him.

"Hey, can one of the two of you get me some PT clothes really quick. About a 2XL please. I've got shoes, but nothing else," Jim said.

The young red-headed soldier looked at him, "You aren't really gonna mess with Rachel, are you?" he spoke incredulously.

"Well, that would be a goal, but I just need to stretch out a bit," Jim smiled.

"Damn, are you stupid?" The redhead looked on. "She is a 3rd degree Black Belt in something. I had to spar her once and she took me down so fast I fainted."

Jim put his arm on the boy's shoulder. "Of course you did," he said with a smile. "That's why you can get me a PT uniform really quick and we can go work out."

Jim walked back into the room and Alex said, "You really are a glutton for punishment, aren't you?"

"Why yes, sleeping beauty," he laughed. "Wanna come watch me get my ass kicked by a girl?"

"Why not," Alex said stretching up, "but you best not be overconfident. I was yesterday and had my ass handed to me."

"Ouch," said Jim. "And here I thought everyone would want a piece of ass. It's just bad when it's yours."

"Cute," Alex almost smiled, "really cute."

"We have twenty minutes," Jim smiled. "That little E1 better not make me late."

"As always, begging for it," Alex took three deep breaths and got up.

A moment later there was a knock on the door and the red-headed private walked in with a bag. "I got ya what I could from supply. I didn't know how to charge it so the corporal may be on my ass..."

Jim broke in, "She will be on my ass first. We'll deal with it." He quickly slipped down to briefs. He was a big man, with a bit of a belly and huge tree trunk arms and legs. With his size, Jim looked like a bear without all the hair. It would be easy to imagine him as fuzzy wuzzy in the old kid's song if he wasn't grinning nearly all the time. He quickly put on the shorts and standard issue t-shirt and sat down to put his Nikes back on.

Jim jumped up and said, "Time to go. Let's move it, little sergeant. Get your butt moving."

Alex was moving slowly, still sore from the previous day's events and less than fully rested. It didn't matter though. He was a Ranger and there were none better. Period. He pushed through and was walking out the door with Jim.

A brief walk outside and they were at the Depot gym. As they walked in, the bright lights illuminated a small group of people warming up.

"She has several warm up with her every morning." the red-haired guard said. "We can go back to the barracks if you like."

Jim looked at him, "You go ahead. Get your teddy bear while you are at it," he smiled.

Alex laughed.

"About time you laugh," Jim said. "I thought I was getting rusty."

"Hey little guy," a commanding woman's voice came, "welcome to my place."

Jim smiled and simply said, "Howdy," as he saw Rachel with red sparring gloves and headgear walking onto a large mat. Several men were dressed in their headgear and gloves as well, but theirs were dark blue. Only the corporal sported the red gear. The gloves allowed some movement, but softened the punch. He looked and saw they had feet pads as well. Apparently it was going to be fun.

"Johnson," she said in a commanding tone as a tall but lanky man straightened to attention automatically. "Strip off that gear and give it to the little guy."

Johnson was overly ready to give up the gear and did so quickly and efficiently while Jim, as quickly and efficiently, took it from him. Johnson apparently was wanting to be out of the gear as much as Jim wanted to be in it.

Jim stripped off his shoes as well and put on the foot covers that would allow for some serious kicks. As he did so, Rachel looked at him and smiled, "You really think you can use those with that belly?"

Jim smiled, "Naw, but I don't know if you can dance yet and don't want you to step on my toesies."

Jim walked onto the mat, stretching as he did. The sparring area was set up to be about forty feet by forty feet and Jim circled slightly as he walked slowly in towards the center of the ring. Rachel circled as well; her size was deceiving as anyone could see she moved like a panther while she kept her eyes focused on Jim.

Alex looked on from the side and wondered how this would go. He had not kept up with Jim like he should have, but in the past Jim was top notch. Now he was older and had put on a little weight, but Alex knew the muscle memory and skill didn't fade easily. As Alex looked around the room, he surveyed the group of soldiers who shuffled in anticipation. It seemed the hope was that they would not have to be next in whatever was to come.

The circled tightened. Jim smiled at Rachel; she smiled back with one of those smiles you see a person make when they know they are in control. Jim's smile changed to a smirk as he knew her overconfidence was immense.

As Jim was within a few feet, Rachel fired a front punch straight at him, at which Jim simply pivoted his body slightly and it passed by. Rachel's pull back was followed by a rapid twist of her body as her arm outstretched long and she tried to backhand him, only to land on air as he again moved out of the way. She pulled back, "Not quite as slow as I thought you would be little guy. All the better."

Three fast punches landed on air again and as the third came towards him, Jim brought his arm down and carried her momentum forward, knocking Rachel off balance. She stumbled and he used the stumble to spin her slightly like Baryshnikov would have in a ballet.

Rachel turned and was slightly red. She slowed herself, quiet now, her overconfidence gone. Three rapid round kicks and all misses, but she followed with a punch that caught Jim in the side of the shoulder.

Jim stepped back, brushed his shoulder and looked at Rachel. "Love tap?" he said. "I'm flattered."

The verbal jab made Rachel's brow furl. Moving forward, she fired a sidearm swing. Jim blocked it instead of letting it pass and this time, stepped into her. With her arm outstretched, he pinned her other arm between them, pulled her close and lifted her off the ground, all in a fraction of a moment. She struggled and was obviously muscular, but Jim kissed her on the cheek and in a quick motion pushed her away.

The men in the room were now clapping as no one had ever been able to deal with the corporal like this. Alex watched and smiled as his old friend did what he used to do best.

Rachel was seriously red now and excited. Her face seemed to seethe like a volcano ready to erupt. Somewhere in that kiss on the cheek she had lost the control she wanted and now she jumped on her toes working her way back to him. Her face was now covered with grim determination. In a rapid move she grabbed Jim's arm and twisted it behind him. Jim seemed to be in trouble. She pushed him in an arm bar towards the ground, but at the last moment Jim twisted back facing her, his strength obviously more than she had anticipated and she fell forward on him. Not in control anymore, he held her arms so she could not balance as they rolled to the ground. Jim shifted and used the momentum to push her all the way over while he rode with the makeshift somersault. When he landed he was on top of her, straddling her chest with her arms pinned under his knees.

"Give up?" he asked her.

The men were laughing now and clapping again and Alex was suitably impressed.

"Hell no," she huffed.

Jim smiled at her and said, "Well, I guess I do."

Jim rolled off of her and was on his feet in a twist kip in a second.

"You are just too good for me," he laughed as he stripped off the gear for his hands, feet and head.

"Get your ass back here," Rachel said with her face red.

Jim laughed, "No no, you win," Jim said with his back to her.

He giggled as he walked out the door with Alex and the two guards that had come with them. The red-headed guard ran behind, bringing Jim's shoes to him.

"That was fun," Jim said as he turned and blew a kiss to the now red-faced corporal he had left at the mat.

Alex looked at Jim as they were leaving and just shook his head. The large door closed behind them as they walked into the morning air.

Chapter 27 – Fluctuation

Michael woke still holding Abby and as he stirred she grabbed his arm and would not let go. Michael's dream disturbed him as he thought he had passed that part of his life. He thought he had let go of what he did and buried any potential guilt with feelings of righteousness and vengeance. He laid there holding Abby, not willing to move. Knowing if he had just not been so selfish his sophomore year, maybe his mother would have left and she would still be alive today. Then again, if she had left, perhaps Michael would still be Jon and would have done something else he thought was right at the time. It was much easier taking the life of someone you didn't know as you could remain disconnected. To Michael, all of his targets had been just that, targets. No more important than the paper targets at the range.

It was that one day long ago that had changed all that. His watching Diana through the scope and hearing her husband had given her a voice; she became a person instead of a target. Since that emotionally charged day, he had avoided his former occupation. Only Abby had made his life complete and though he was constantly working on his skills, he had not thought he would use them in the same way again.

Michael slid slowly away from Abby and she groaned. He got off his side of the bed and treaded lightly like an invisible giant cat. Glancing at the clock he knew it would be 4:00AM and it was exactly that. He stretched for a moment, his washboard abs glistening in the dim light. Michael reached into a drawer and pulled out a pair of sweatpants with the tag still on them. He ripped off the tag, put on the sweats and went down to the rec room.

Having a good workout was at the core of each one of Michael's days. Normally he worked out on the bag, cardio, then weights, but yesterday was full of excitement and didn't allow him as much passion and focus as he usually had for his workout.

Michael started working with easy dumbbells and worked himself into a sweat with only forty pounds on each arm. After about ten minutes, he began a series of stretches and poses that allowed him to stay limber, then moved to a treadmill and began a fast run.

The whole workout took a little over an hour, but Michael felt refreshed and in control. Putting a fresh towel over his neck, he walked to the wall and opened the door to his hidden room.

As the computers came on, he glanced at the weapons still on the floor and decided to take care of stowing them first. The walls were not quite full in these cases, but the basics were here. Michael opened a series of drawers and pulled out several rags and cans and moved them to the side. He then pulled out a thin drawer that actually turned out to be a makeshift table about five-feet-long, at a comfortable working level.

Michael opened each bag he had brought, verified the weapon status, wiped the weapon down, then opened a case and mounted the weapon in its place. Within twenty minutes, he had stowed all of the weapons he had brought, except two. Michael stopped for a moment and put the P90 and the FN Five-seven on the table protruding from the wall.

With careful ease, Michael broke both weapons into their individual pieces. In mere moments they went from lethal weapons to steel and "Tupperware". Michael pulled out little tools from the cases he had set out and began cleaning all of the pieces and in less time than it would take a normal person to do the dishes, had cleaned both weapons and began to rapidly reassemble them. Satisfied, he smiled as he looked down at his two weapons of choice.

Michael then cleaned his table area and put the weapons in their cases, discarded the used rags and stored his tools. Opening a small drawer, he took out another rag and cleaned the area. Though no one could easily see anything, there was grime as he wiped areas down and in a short time the room was clean. Michael then pushed the makeshift table back into its place in the wall and smiled again.

He was now cooling down, so he walked to the computers that had come online when he first walked in. The message light flashed, so

Michael pressed a few buttons and brought up the messages as he had the day before. A message from an unknown number flashed.

Michael clicked play and a computer voice began speaking.

"Michael," the computer voice stated, "for your safety, stay out of it. As I promised, I am watching. Wyoming is nice."

Michael looked at the system and thought. No one could know where they were. Or could they?

Chapter 28 – Intentions

After a shower and a shave, Alex and Jim headed to the mess with their circling guard of newbies. Going through the well-run line, they grabbed breakfast in the less than crowded mess hall. Most of the crews had long since been up, ate and been on to working on bigger and better things.

After getting much needed coffee and sitting at the table, they became somewhat of a spectacle. After all, Jim was now the base hero as the person who had bested Rachel in her morning workout and certainly saved at least one poor schmuck from a morning embarrassment.

As Jim sipped coffee and laughed at Alex, Rachel walked up with a tray and stood next to the table. Jim looked up.

"May I sit down?" she said in a mock polite voice.

Jim looked up and said, "Sure," then paused, "you wanna have an eating contest now?"

Rachel sat down and pulled her chair close to the table. She was much more mild mannered than she had been before. "I tend to get a little carried away," she began. "I always want to be the best. I looked you up after the beating you could have put on me. You could have told me you were a grandmaster."

"Old news," said Jim, "and never really official. Besides, you never let me get a word in edgewise."

"Official enough for your record," Rachel said. "Anyway, I am sorry if I offended you. I know I am over the top, but it is not true to the art for me to be that way."

"It is fun, though," Jim said, "and life is about having fun."

Everyone in the room jumped up as the door opened and General Sam Tarkington walked into the room.

"At ease you idiots," the general said as he walked to the table where Jim sat and Alex stood. The general looked at Jim. "Still bucking the system?" he asked.

Jim flashed a quick salute to him, but didn't get up. "You're still the system?" Jim said looking back to his plate.

"That I am. With me, you two," the general stated dryly and turned walking towards the door.

"I think you missed the part where I am no longer under your command," Jim said.

The general tapped his aide on the arm who ran forward and handed Jim a stack of papers.

"I think you will find that you are mine again. You have been reinstated, got the President's signature and all. Now move your ass," the general barked.

Jim got up and sauntered towards the direction of the general like a whipped puppy with a bad bone, while Alex walked in a pure formation.

"Damnit Alex, this just isn't right," Jim said.

"Just tell him you don't know anything and you will be fine," Alex said as they walked to the door and out into the cold morning air once again.

Chapter 29 – Compulsion

Michael was up, dressed and in a loose-fitting set of cargo pants and tee shirt before Abby really started moving. As he was finishing brushing his teeth, she strolled into the marble floored bathroom and hugged him from behind. Swiveling, he turned and hugged her back and reached down to kiss her.

Abby covered her mouth and said, "Morning breath."

Michael laughed. "Doesn't matter," he said and moved her hand aside to kiss her. "A kiss from you is always sweet."

Abby kissed him back and as they broke the kiss said, "Eww, that was just too sweet and sappy. I am not sure if I should throw up from that comment or if you should, from my breath."

They both laughed together and he hugged her.

He looked back at the mirror with a semi sullen brow.

"What's wrong?" Abby queried.

Michael smiled, "Nothing."

"Liar," she teased. "You promised to never lie to me, ever."

"Sorry," Michael said with true sincerity. "I got another message from a strange caller. It was well concealed and a computer synthesized voice. It says once again I should not do whatever I think I should do."

"Who do you think it is?" Abby asked.

"I really don't know," Michael said. "The only time I ever got something similar was several years ago after my father died."

"Think it is the same person?" Abby asked.

"Seems different. Different voice, but voice engines have changed a lot over the years," Michael said dryly.

"What did it say then?" Abby asked.

"It said it was not you, don't feel guilty," Michael said. "I never knew what it meant."

Abby paused, "Do you think it was something to do with someone else? Your dad or your mom? Something completely unrelated?"

Michael shrugged slightly, "I have thought about it for years. I really don't know."

Abby smiled and hugged Michael, "I am sure you will know what to do. You always do."

Michael hugged her back and as he held her he thought about the caller.

The door pounded. "What are you two doing in there?" He heard Jay say from behind it. Abby closed the bathroom door as Michael walked to the door and opened it.

"Dressed," Michael said, "let's go talk. Maybe I can convince Abby to make breakfast." Michael raised his voice. "Abby, can you make some breakfast? Won't be much here, but do what you can."

Michael walked with Jay, who had obviously also gotten a shower and gotten dressed. They headed downstairs as Michael explained his potential plan.

"I want to get somewhere far away from here so Abby will be okay. I am not sure what is going on, but I am sure it is not as cut and dried as it seems. Too many people came too fast. I need to get to South Korea first and see what I can figure out about Karen. Then I need to find out what is going on with our beloved government, if they are really looking for me or if something else is going on. It would be best if I can do both at once."

Jay nodded. "You really have not told me what the hell is going on, so maybe you should back up for a second and bring me up to speed."

"Not super necessary," Michael said. "I am pretty sure we will have plenty of time to talk in the air. I think we should all talk first though, so everyone is on the same page."

"Good point. Should I go get everyone?" Jay said.

"I need to pull some intel to read on the way and if we go, we need a few weapons to hide in your plane," Michael said.

Jay laughed. "Yep, I was pretty sure of that. Knowing you, I bet you put them all away and cleaned them all last night. Never did know anyone who kept his damn guns so clean."

"Always upset me when I was young and my dad didn't clean his weapons for months," Michael said solemnly.

"Big sin," Jay said.

"Smallest of the ones I know of," Michael said, "but it had its effect on me."

"Ever think of seeing a shrink for the OCD?" Jay asked.

"I could tell him why I was so OCD…" Michael shifted into a gruff gangster voice, "but then I'd have to kill em."

Jay laughed as they reached Michael's secret room. "He turned at the weight bench and said, "I will go upstairs and get everyone together and ask Abby about breakfast. Can you come up and talk to us and then let's get this show on the road?"

Michael nodded and walked into his room as Jay spun around, "Yeah, you go to your room and I will go back up the damn stairs. Seems I am always going up and down stairs."

"You could get a smaller plane," Michael laughed.

"Not happening," Jay said as he headed back up.

As Michael walked into the room and the lights and computers came on he thought to himself, "This room is not much of a secret this week."

Chapter 30 – Transformation

The white walls in the room washed into the white tile floor. The older oak table in the center of the room was a huge contrast and Alex was irritated by it. He looked around as Jim leaned back in his rickety oak chair and stared at the white tiles in the ceiling.

"God, I hate these ceilings," Jim said with obvious disdain. "There aren't even any bugs in the room, they are too afraid to come in here."

Alex looked at Jim, "Really?"

Jim looked at Alex, "Yeah, they are probably afraid they will get cussed to death if the general comes in."

Alex laughed, "Probably true."

The door swung open and the general walked in.

"Alex, I just read your official report. It smells like fucking shit. What did you pick, retards to go in with you? Yeah, yeah, I know, the little fuckers are dead, but two people were hogtied before you even knew what was going on? I am sad for their families, knowing you killed their children because you couldn't lead yourself into a warm pile of shit if you were in a field of it. Now you need to choose your next words damn well boy, because I can't see how you can tell me this is anything but a fuck up. I know this spook ass shithead is missing and he will get a piece of me too. I need to know why you were so ineffective. Then I need to know what the fuck we are going to do about this. And how."

Jim laughed.

"...and you, you big fucker. That's right. I know you are still a bad ass, but you are still my little bad ass. You need to shut the fuck up. You drove to the middle of nowhere to pick this asshole up and didn't call anyone? I should throw your fucking ass in Gitmo and let it rot for..."

"Enough," Alex stood rapidly and slammed his fists on the table. "I know I may be court martialed after this, but you need to shut up and listen. I had good men, damn good men and you just treated them with disrespect. We were all tops, but we were not briefed and we probably should not have been there at all. Think about it, you over cussing piece of shit. We went in and this man let us live. HE LET US LIVE. So why would he do that? He was actually nice to us. Why would he do that? You are asking the wrong questions and we are wasting time and energy just sitting here with you. We need to figure out what the fuck is going on or we are going to see some major issues. Now let's talk about how we are going to fix this and talk about the American fucking missiles that killed my people right after my sat phone call."

Tarkington sat down. He was quiet and looked at the table. He reached into his front pocket and pulled out a cigar. He lit it and leaned his head back, sucking in air and making the tip of the cigar glow bright red. As Alex stood still resolute, he puffed the cigar and a small cloud of smoke formed. A guard walked up to the general and whispered something into his ear, to which the general looked over and said, "Fuck you" and took another puff. "Move your ass back to the corner."

"Welcome back, sergeant," Tarkington said. "I was getting tired of that pussy Alex."

Jim started laughing out loud. "Yeah, me too. Mopey little bastard, isn't he?"

The general glanced in an angry manner at Jim, then turned to Alex, "So what is our move?"

Alex was under control and still strategic. "Well, first things first. We need to find out who killed my men. I am sure it wasn't Masterson. I am of the mind it was friendly. Second, we need to find out where this twit girl found out how to find Masterson and find a way to find him now. Third, we need to determine what North Korea's involvement was and I can guarantee it was North Korea and last, we need to get our asses in gear with people we can trust so we can move forward instead of hiding from each other."

"People we can trust, huh?" the general said as he took a deep puff on his cigar and stood. He looked at the guard who had whispered to him earlier and blew the smoke his way. "Okay Alex, pick your team, but I suggest you put this little shit on it." The general flicked his cigar at Jim who caught it in mid-air. "I want you in planning in two hours to get me answers. Make it happen, sergeant."

Tarkington walked out of the room and left Jim and Alex alone.

Chapter 31 – Oration

Michael stood looking out the windows over the amazing mountain view. The crisp colors of morning and light mist in the air made the area look almost surreal and as inviting as any place in the world. As he stared out, a hawk drifted in the air slowly floating by the windows. In an instant the hawk dove deep to some unseen quarry below and Michael knew that the hunter who waits, as this hawk did, could see the bigger picture and was usually successful.

He turned around at the den area where Janet, Jay, Madison and his beloved Abby sat watching him.

"It is hard to say how this will go," he began. "This whole thing has gotten out of hand and I am not sure where to get information I can trust. I can tell you that someone else is involved and I am not sure who they are, government or individual. I have been asked not to be involved. I have been asked to be involved, but I am not sure what the question really is yet, as most of the information is little more than anecdotal."

Michael paused a moment. "The point is Madison, I really do not know if your mom is dead or alive and there seems to be little information of value out there to lead me to believe one way or another. The videos I have found are real, but they could have been taken in North Korea, South Korea or Kansas and making a decision without good intelligence may well be suicide, just like your mercenaries told you."

"Not my...," Madison started and Michael waved a hand and cut her off.

"If I am to help," Michael continued, "I need to be sure I know what I am up against. Otherwise I am dead. Or worse." He looked at Madison with a solemn visage, "There are things worse than death."

"I got another message last night, which means at least one person knows how to get to me, but nothing is happening on that front. So here is what we know. We know the American government wants to talk to me. I am not sure if it is in a positive or negative manner and I let their representatives go, without a heavy fight. We know that North Korean soldiers were here, but they were not necessarily from the North Korean government. They could be from North Korea, but not really on orders. We have no proof."

"But they…," Madison started, but Michael again waved her off.

Michael continued. "We know little else at this point. Your files are not complete, nor do we have any real government statement on anything. What we have from the government is so well written it looks almost staged, which makes me wary."

Michael looked at Jay and Janet who seemed mesmerized at Michael's melodic analysis. "Jay, I am not sure I want you in the middle of all of this, but I don't trust many others. I think you should talk to Janet alone for a moment. If you are good with helping, we will leave the girls here and head out this morning after breakfast. I will need to pack a few things. It will be better if they do not know where we are going, but we will keep in touch. and Abby knows how safe this house can be."

"As safe as the last one," Abby smiled, "and still half mine." She winked at Michael.

Michael smiled and continued, "Madison, you will need to stay here, too. I don't need you in the middle of this and you are the weakest link in the chain. Janet, Abby and Jay have been through this, while you only know the tip of the iceberg. "

"But what if you need me?" Madison started.

"For what?" Michael said. "To distract me, keep me from seeing the bigger picture? To give me another blind spot or to bleed on me and ruin one of my nice shirts? Be real Madison, you asked for my help. It is like this. I do this my way or you walk out of here and hitchhike back to Kentucky and disappear, for all I care."

Madison started crying.

Abby looked at her. "Stop it Madison. You know Michael is right," then glaring at Michael, "even though he seems to be a little too harsh about it."

Michael laughed. "Abby, this could be it. Don't coddle her. She needs to know the danger she has put us all in." He looked at Jay and Janet, "You two go talk for a few."

Janet jumped in. "We already have. Jay and I would not be alive if it wasn't for you or at least not together. Jay will help and I will too, if you need it."

Michael looked into her chocolate brown eyes and saw the sincerity she was beaming to him. "Thank you. I can ask Jay, but I want you safe too. I will get him back to you or at least keep him out of harm's way."

Janet looked at Jay. "I appreciate that. Don't let him look at another woman either."

Jay laughed. "You know better," he said with his hands up in a scout's honor salute. "I only want you in my life."

Michael stopped, looked at Abby. "Abby, if you say no, I will not do this. You are my life and I will never do anything you don't want me to do."

Abby looked at him, small tears welled up in her eyes. "You know you have to and I know you have to. Not for Madison, but because it's the right thing."

Michael smiled and said simply, "Let's eat."

Chapter 32 – Identification

Jim was still just plain pissed off. "I would rather be doing anything than helping him again." Jim paused a moment, then continued, "I mean, he crapped on my life and I am supposed to take it?"

Alex was more in control. His burst of anger had given him the cool resolution he had on the mountain, after Michael had humbled him and someone had betrayed him. "Jim, I know, but help me get this done and we'll move on."

"You guys really know the general," the red-haired guard shadowing them said. "I mean, like personally."

Jim made a face that looked straight out of the movie Valley Girl. "Yep, we know him like personally, like wow, like he is so like just really like radically stupid. What's your name kid?"

"Ronnie, sir," the boy said, not even noticing Jim's sarcasm, "Ronnie Comer."

"Well, Private Ronnie Comer," Jim started, "Do you know the general and how bad he has messed up some of our lives? No? Well then why don't you just shut up for a second? Why don't you put this genius on your team and let me go home, Alex?"

"I need four, at least and I have you. So I might as well." Alex looked at Comer and asked, "Where you from, boy?"

"Harlan, Kentucky, sir," Ronnie said proudly.

"Okay Ronnie from Harlan. Go find Corporal Brown and get her to …," Alex paused, "…where do we find the meeting rooms?"

"On the hill, sir, just up there a piece," Ronnie pointed.

Jim laughed, "Yep, up thar a piece."

Alex glared at him and continued, "Ronnie, get Brown and get up there. I will secure a room. We need to talk."

Ronnie scurried off like an overactive bloodhound in search of a scent.

Jim looked at him, "You aren't thinking..."

Alex looked at him. "Yes, I am. I don't know who I can trust right now. So I have you, a kid from Harlan and a girl with too much pride to be compromised. Maybe we will have a chance to get out of this alive."

Jim laughed. "Well, maybe it will be fun, but I doubt we will get out alive with Tarkington in control."

"Maybe," Alex sighed, "but I want out alive and I don't want to lose anyone else. We need answers for Tarkington to let any of us go and we need to figure out how and where to get them from."

As they reached the door to the central building that Ronnie had pointed to, Jim grabbed and opened it. "Do you have any idea how we will accomplish this little miracle?"

"Yes, I do," Alex began. "We will start by identifying a geek somewhere in this building, maybe let Ronnie find him and start working backwards from Michael and whoever sent us out. It would be nice to find Michael and figure out exactly what is going on, but that may well take a miracle."

"I stopped believing in miracles a long time ago," Jim said dryly. "But as long as I am stuck here, I might as well go down the rabbit hole with you."

They reached a reception desk and Alex asked for a room. The young soldier sitting at the desk was pretty and looked up and said, "Yes, sir, it has already been arranged. Down the hall to your right." She handed them envelopes. "These are your identification cards, papers and a voucher to get whatever you need for uniforms and extras. Do you need anything else?"

Jim looked at her glowing hazel eyes and tightly wrapped red hair in a bun. He glanced to the nameplate which simply said, "Templeton".

"Well Miss Templeton, now that you ask," he said in a voice close to the Pepe LePew character in Looney Tunes days.

"Let's move," Alex said.

As they walked down the hall to the conference room Jim mumbled, "You are just no fun, no fun at all."

Behind them the red-headed young woman smiled after Jim thinking unknown thoughts.

Chapter 33 – Exasperation

Breakfast in Wyoming was amazing as the group looked out upon the spectacular view of the mountains. Occasionally birds would fly by, adding to the ambiance. Michael was cordial to the group, but not his usually talkative self and frequently reached under the table and gave Abby's leg a soft squeeze as if to reassure her he was still there. Abby smiled each time and grabbed his hand and held it tightly for a moment.

As they finished their breakfast, Michael stood up with Abby and hugged her tightly, then made his way downstairs again. He had already packed the papers he needed and a pair of small tablet computers, a set of chargers and a bag containing basic weapons. Michael knew that, depending on where they ended up, he would have to acquire weapons if he needed more than the basics. Michael took his bags to the Suburban and then went back into the not so secret room for one last pass. As he was about to shut down the computer, he noticed the message light was again flashing.

"Again?" Michael actually uttered aloud.

He hit play on the message. There was a bit of space in this one, then a computer voice simply said, "Be wary."

Michael shut the system down and walked out of the room, sealing it behind him. He walked up the stairs to the den.

Jay was waiting with a bag and a smile. As usual he was jovial and animated as he hugged Janet, then Abby and Madison. Janet glared and Jay hugged her again. She smiled and said, "Just kidding."

Abby laughed and Michael hugged her tightly and kissed her passionately.

Jay laughed, "Get a room," as Michael broke the kiss and they all laughed with him for a moment.

Madison stepped forward and grabbed Michael's hand. "Thank you for whatever happens."

"Such confidence," Michael said dryly. "Let's go, Jay."

Abby once again said, "Be careful."

Michael looked at her, turned slightly and danced up and down.

"Yes, it's still mine," Abby said.

"I know," Michael smiled as he and Jay headed to the staircase. "I will keep it safe. Me and Jay, too."

They disappeared down the stairs to the garage.

Jay looked at Michael as he climbed in to the Suburban. "Are we up for this?"

"I am," Michael said, "but if you are not you can just stay here."

"And have you take my plane?" Jay said comically. "I don't think so."

"Well," Michael started as they backed out of the garage, "I can fly it as well as you can."

"Takes two baby," Jay said. "Well at least to do it right."

Michael grinned, "Sure, whatever. You are just getting soft flying around crooks and sheiks."

"I would never fly crooks around," Jay said.

"Sure you would," Michael said, "but I bet that plane eats gas."

"You don't know the half of it brother," Jay said as they started down the hill.

It would be a while before they got to the plane and Michael was silent, considering his next move.

Chapter 34 – Combination

Private Comer came into the conference room meekly and said, "I found her," as Corporal Brown pushed past almost knocking down the private.

She looked at the two men and said, "What is this all about?"

"Pardon, corporal?" Alex started. "You are in the presence of two Master Sergeants."

Rachel stopped, looked at them and said, "What?"

Alex showed her the credentials and Jim opened his as well in a less than official manner.

Rachel snapped to attention, "Master Sergeants."

"At ease, Rachel." Alex started. "This is going to sound strange and you are about to be read into something big." Comer was still standing at the door and was walking out starting to close it when Jim stopped him.

"Get in here, boy," Jim said in a very southern voice, "This is for you, too."

"Sir?" Comer asked.

"Sit your bottom down at the table and listen up," Jim said again.

"Yes sir," Comer sat down nervously as Rachel and Alex looked on.

Alex continued, "You may not be aware of why we are here, in fact, you better not be. Yesterday morning at about 0600 we were dropped into a LZ near Ivel, Kentucky from intel on a woman the CIA had been monitoring, at that point to detain a supposed non-com. Upon entry, my men were forcibly detained as well as myself and my second in command. It got dicey and we were released when four North Koreans approached the location with the same target. It appeared we were utilized as bait and the non-com detained the four easily and though letting us roam, disarmed myself and my second."

"Sir, Ivel is a ways out from anywhere. Who was this guy?" Comer asked.

Rachel glared at the private for interrupting, but Alex said, "Good question. I will get there in a moment."

"The non-com questioned the North Koreans in our presence and killed one brutally to get answers. It was apparent he was professional and we were far outgunned. The tactics he used were not standard, nor was his skill at shooting. At several points he displayed accuracy that was beyond most civilians and most servicemen. He also displayed high proficiency with edged weapons," Alex continued.

"We have identified the non-com as Jonathon Michael Masterson. His parents have been dead for several years. His mother died in a freak accident caused by his father. He blamed his father for the death, but the courts didn't agree. His father was killed leaving the courthouse by a 50-caliber rifle. It was suspected Jonathon killed his own father, but nothing could be proven. At that point Jonathon dropped off the grid after he graduated with an engineering degree." Alex paused and took a drink from a bottle of water.

"The file is not fully accurate, but it appears Jonathon had begun taking private assassination jobs somewhere in college and by the time he graduated had amassed a major fortune, including paying off his school debts which we know can be considerable." Alex paused for a second and smiled, then looked at them all.

"Interviews from schoolmates said that he was a good student and a changed person after his mother died, taking on the name Michael instead of Jonathon. Given it took over a year for his father's trial, he had a lot of time in between the two deaths. The CIA apparently had utilized him at several times, unconfirmed, and various groups around the world until about three years ago when a job went bad or there was some misunderstanding and Michael terminated the wrong target." Alex stopped.

"I have been in many situations, but never have I felt as outgunned as I did yesterday. It wasn't what he did, it was the complete nonchalant attitude he had. We were less than an inconvenience and maybe even a pleasant diversion," Alex said softly.

Returning to his strong voice, "At any rate, we were released with the prisoners, only to have our transport blown up after reporting in by unknown missiles. I was the only one who survived."

Rachel interjected, "Then why should we trust you?"

Jim glared, "Because …"

Alex stopped him. "It's okay." Alex looked at Rachel. "You either will eventually or will not. I will do everything I can to keep my team safe."

"Your team?" Rachel asked.

"The two of you and Jim will be the new team. Our job will be to figure out who killed my men, why Michael or Jonathon or whatever his name is was targeted and to determine actions and execute as necessary," Alex said.

"I asked you both here because I feel I have a blank slate and neither of you is compromised in any way. If you don't want the job, speak now. If you do, we have work to do."

"So where do we start?" Rachel asked.

"Yeah, what can I do?" Ronnie asked.

"Ronnie," Alex said, "I need someone who knows computers. Get someone on base that can start looking up some things for us and get them into this room."

Alex looked at Jim and Rachel. "You two go through these files." Alex moved a banker's box of files to the center of the table. "Find something we can use or some pattern he has so we can find him."

"What about you?" Jim asked.

"He had to get out of town after he blew his house up." Alex said. "I am going to look for a plane or something that could have gotten him out of here. Anything odd I can find."

Jim laughed. "So Ronnie has the easy job while the rest of us search for needles in haystacks."

"Basically," Alex said. "So get searching."

The team started digging in to what was available. Alex was on a mission, a mission to find out what killed his men and whether Michael was friend or foe.

Chapter 35 – Assumption

The airport was booming with people looking at the massive plane. The appearance of the monstrosity was probably the biggest thing that had happened in this city for a long time. The plane with its massive photo on the side was a rarity in itself, but at an airport with such a small community it was even more of a spectacle.

"I guess the request for privacy wasn't high on their list," Michael stated.

"They just love my little Scotsman," Jay smiled.

"A bit over the top, don't you think," Michael stated dryly.

"About as bad as me," Jay said.

"Amen," said Michael. "Amen."

The two drove into the gates and up to the front of the massive plane where Jay jumped out and parted the crowd like Moses parting the Red Sea. Jay entered on the side at the hatch and moments later the tail of plane lowered and the skids came down for the vehicle to drive up.

The crowd clapped in appreciation and Michael rolled his eyes in the Suburban. As the ramp came down, Michael began driving up towards the tail of the plane, then as the ramp hit ground, he rolled up into the belly of the C130J Hercules.

The crowd was still clapping and the massive plane began to close as Jay walked up to the cockpit. Moments later the huge engines began spinning up and the crowd retreated to the safety behind the fences. The sound was deafening and many of the spectators covered their ears and walked backwards.

Michael locked down the truck, then went up to the cockpit and sat in the co-pilot's seat. He put the headset on after adjusting it from an obviously smaller persons head. Hitting the internal mic button, he said, "Think you can get this thing off the ground on this short runway?"

"I would assume so; I stopped it on this short runway," Jay said.

Michael laughed. "Taking off on an assumption," he said to Jay on the com channel. Michael keyed the radio, "This is GYZa55 Heavy. Request permission for takeoff."

"GYZa55 Heavy," the voice on the radio came, "umm, we don't think you can get your plane off the ground."

Jay keyed his mic. "I got it down here, I will get it out of here. Have you got anything coming down? This thing can take off in your backyard if it needs to."

"No, but no one thinks you can do this," the voice came.

"This is GYZa55 Heavy, taxiing to runway end. By the way, get some better advisors, then watch and learn," Jay said as the huge engines whined even more and the plane began moving. After less than two minutes, the monumental plane that dwarfed the small rural tower had moved to the far end of the runway.

Jay looked at Michael. "You ready for this?"

Michael looked back. "Sure. Abby always wanted the house. I'm just glad she doesn't know about the other one."

Jay keyed the mic again. "This is GYZa55 Heavy, bye-bye."

Jay slammed down the brakes and flaps hard and spun up the engines. The wheels tried to move, but the oversized pads held firm. The engines whined even more and the wheels began skidding forward slowly, even as the brakes tried desperately to grip the ground like the Looney Tunes coyote held onto the cliffs edge. Jay looked at the engines and pressed the throttles more and waited for just a second longer, then dropped the brakes.

The giant plane lurched forward as if pushed by the hand of some immense being and began rocketing down the runway. Michael sat back as Jay continued to throttle up higher until the engines bellowed with the thunder of a thousand storms.

Jay watched the gauges and the runway and the runway seemed to shrink even faster than the speed increased for them.

"We're not going to make it," Michael said though the mic.

Jay started laughing almost hysterically and for a moment Michael thought they were lost until Jay pulled back on the wheel and the massive plane shattered the bond of gravity and soared into the air.

"Were you saying something?" Jay asked as the plane continued to gain altitude. The plane had taken off several thousand feet in front of the limit, something no one but a pilot would understand. The C130J Hercules was made to take off from just about anywhere and Jay knew the plane better than most.

"Me? Nope. Not me," Michael said in a mock meek voice.

Jay laughed, then the laugh turned into a wild semi-insane howl.

"God, please don't do that," Michael said. "You set the flight plan?"

"Filed for Tokyo via Portland," Jay stated. "Hope you got your passport."

"Sounds good," Michael said.

Jay stated, "We will deal with everything else when we get to Tokyo."

The "Happy Scotsman" headed west towards Portland. And answers.

Chapter 36 – Computation

Alex was impressed. Rachel and Jim had actually overcome some of the early frustrations and after Rachel called Jim an "ignorant hypocritical sexist bigot" they both had a big laugh and finally meshed like Alex thought they would.

Ronnie had fulfilled his quest and found a technician who was busy scanning FAA registrations, takeoff and landings. It didn't take long for Tony Dickson, a thin overly tattooed computer guru, to find a plane in the wrong place, at the wrong time. The aircraft was far too large for the airport that it landed at. The C130J Hercules was impressive and only a few were in use outside of the Armed Forces.

Huntington, West Virginia, was an airport barely capable of dealing with mid-sized aircraft, but the logs clearly showed the massive plane, "The Lucky Scotsman", landing at the airport and leaving just minutes later. The flight plan upon leaving was set for Salt Lake City; however, the plane didn't land there and instead fell off the grid for a short time. A blog post from a small town in Wyoming told the story as the plane was again spotted there overnight. A YouTube video of the massive plane taking off from an airport too small for the plane finished the story and was only an hour old. The flight plan for the plane was entered as Tokyo, Japan via Portland, Oregon.

Ronnie and Jim whistled, making Jim look over at the young man and grimace. Rachel looked at Jim and said, "So what now?"

"Up to the boss," and looked at Alex.

Rachel looked at Alex and said, "Well, it is out of the country now or it will be in a very short time. So what do we do?"

Alex considered for a moment, then picked up his cell phone and called the general.

"General," Alex started, "We have potentially identified the transport Masterson is using. We are aware this transport is heading out of country. The assumption is they are heading to Japan."

"Go on," said the general.

"I would like permission to attempt interception in Japan and at least try to find out what is going on," Alex continued.

There was a pause at the other end of the phone, muffled discussions were going on until Alex heard, "I said fucking now."

The general came back on the phone. "Alex, get to the Bluegrass Airport in Lexington, Kentucky, ASAP. I have a plane incoming for you. You have forty-five minutes. Make it happen," the general said.

"Yes sir," Alex said.

"Boy, I can't stress enough that this needs to be handled properly. No bullshit and no more deaths. We have bypassed a shitload of paperwork hiding you down there, so prove my gut right and find this guy. And get me answers," the general barked.

Alex returned, "Yes sir."

Alex paused, "Who should go? I am assuming just me."

The general laughed. "You think I let you put this together so you could leave this team in the silo? You will take them with you and train on the job under fire. Make this happen boy."

"But sir, this should be my risk," Alex started.

"Boy," the general broke in, "don't be a dipshit. You will need a team and you need to rely on them. I expect them to be a team by the time you land or shortly after."

"Yes sir," Alex said in a resigned voice.

"Damn straight," the general said and hung up the phone.

"So," Jim said with the others looking on, "What's up?"

Alex looked at each of them, sighed, then stood straight. "Gear up. We have to be at BG Airport in forty-four minutes."

Ronnie piped up, "Uh, it's a thirty-minute drive, sir."

"Then you better get your gear fast and get your ass to the Camaro," Alex stated. "We are out of here in ten. That goes for all of you."

Rachel and Ronnie ran out of the room to get gear while Jim looked at Alex. "Wherever we are going, I am going to need a change of clothes."

"Me too," Alex stated, picking up what little he had in the room. "Me too."

Chapter 37 – Acceleration

It's not that Bluegrass Airport was small, it was just not an Atlanta, a Chicago or even a Greater Cincinnati Airport located in Northern Kentucky. It was a nice airport that had undergone a variety of upgrades over the years; added a parking structure, valet parking, a nice food shop and a new wing to service the plethora of connection flights there.

The private side of the airport boasted a few flight schools and some areas that could be used for the big planes that came in for horse auctions with their near limitless money, class and Americanized attitudes.

It was in this private side that Alex and his team arrived, five minutes early, looking for a flight to take them to Japan in short order. Nothing seemed to be evident until a middle-aged man walked up to the group and said, "Sergeant Brown?"

Alex was a little confused and said, "Yes, that is me."

"Come with me, sir." He turned and led them forward to one of the hangars.

The open hangar doors allowed them to walk in and see the glimmering Gulfstream G650. Alex was aware of the aircraft and knew it was capable of flying 7,000 nautical miles nonstop at speeds of up to Mach 0.925, giving them just what they needed to get to Tokyo, but he had not expected the luxury they had been given.

"Please take the equipment you need inside. I can stow the rest as you require. You four, my co-pilot and one attendant are all that will be on board, so we will have room," the pilot stated.

Alex held out his hand, "Alex Brown."

The man took his hand and said, "Yes sir, I have been briefed while inbound. I also know your team and we have been read into the situation. My name is Captain Terry Drake, your co-pilot is Captain Lisa

Cortez and your flight attendant and backup pilot is Barbara Stone. The general was very pointed, so I really think we should be wheels up ASAP. We can talk more once we are cruising."

"Of course," Alex said. "Let's move guys, on board now."

The small group moved up the stairs quickly and got on board, followed by the pilot urging them forward like a mother hen urges her chicks. Once the group was on board the forward door folded into the plane and Captain Drake worked his way into the cockpit, followed by Co-Pilot Cortez. The door closed as the team began stowing their gear in bins with the help of Barbara Stone.

Alex heard the engines whine and saw Ronnie look around.

"What's wrong private?" Alex asked.

"Just not used to flying very much, sir," Ronnie said.

"Have you flown much?" Alex asked.

"Sir, no sir," Ronnie stated. "Only for the service so far and only when I had to go through basic and chute training sir."

"So this will be your longest flight ever?" Jim said.

"Umm, yes sir," Ronnie said as the plane slowly moved forward. "Yes sir. How long will we be in here?"

Alex looked at Barbara, "How long to Tokyo?"

"About ten hours, sir," Barbara said.

"Holy shee-it," Ronnie said. "That's a long time."

A voice came over the intercom. "We are sliding up to the runway guys and gals. Please strap in and we will get this show on the road. The net and phones will be online once we're airborne."

Barbara helped them strap in and helped Ronnie for a moment more. "Don't worry," she said, "it will be a fun flight."

"Yes Ma'am," he said, even though Barbara was barely older than he was. She was maybe twenty-seven, with long tan legs showing from her thin pencil skirt. Her cotton button up shirt accentuated her near perfect body and her bright hazel eyes gleamed like an autumn breeze under her fiery red hair. Ronnie noticed all this and began to sweat a little. "Thank you, ma'am," he said in a semi-embarrassed tone.

Jim had sat behind Alex as they all had their own rows with the limited passengers. He leaned up to him and said, "Boy's got himself a bit of a crush," and Alex turned to see Ronnie looking at Barbara in a rather embarrassed way, like a fifth grader looks at the beautiful teacher.

Alex smiled and turned his head towards Jim. "It will be a fun flight then."

Alex spoke louder to Barbara. "I need tracking on the target plane as soon as we are up and a set of times showing how long they will be down before we are as well."

Barbara nodded, "Yes sir. We can log on to central when we are up and determine it all. We have determined they will have to stop for fuel at least once."

"Would be nice if we could get to Tokyo first," Alex said.

"Cut them some slack," Jim said, "they have a five-hour head start."

The engines roared as the pilots must have gotten clearance and they cruised down the runway. Alex looked over at Ronnie as his knuckles gripped the fine leather seat he was in. Alex smiled. That had been him a long time ago.

The plane lifted off the ground effortlessly and they turned to speed towards Japan.

Chapter 38 – Inclination

The C130J continued towards Portland, stopping for fuel to make the trip to Japan. Michael was seated in the co-pilot's seat reading over material and looking at his satellite phone and computer. After almost forty-five minutes, he looked to Jay.

"This just doesn't make sense," Michael began. "In a perfect world we would be able to find something out about where Karen is currently. But where I am now is no farther than where we were when I first looked up everything that was going on. I'm not so sure why we are being chased, why Madison was followed or why Karen was even a target to begin with. I should have taken more time with the North Koreans and found out who sent them and what the hell was going on."

"We are going to have to be very careful as we go into Japan. I am not sure what is waiting for us, nor am I really sure if North Korea or anyone else is involved at all. I said that before, but it is becoming more and more confusing as I look at the players and the plays in this weird game," Michael continued.

"I looked as deeply into everything I could at the State Department. So there is a lot of information about Karen and Madison, but there is no definitive link to North Korea," Michael went on.

He paused for a moment. "I simply am not sure where to look now. I am going to make some phone calls while we are flying and try to determine if this next step is a good step at all."

Jay looked at Michael and smiled. "It would be much easier if you could just shoot someone, huh?"

Michael was sullen. "I am not sure that I am really enjoy shooting people anymore. I am also not sure that I don't enjoy shooting people. It is just always easier when you know where your target is, just in case they are behind you."

Jay laughed again. "Yea, I know what you mean. It's like that old picture that I used to look at of all the fish chasing each other. There's no such thing as a free lunch."

Michael smiled for a moment. "I agree. I am just not sure who is at the back of this slew of fish yet."

Jay looked at Michael with some seriousness. "You always had a plan before. Even when you should not have, you had a plan and were given a target and intel. This is different. With all your limitless intelligence, you need to now understand how someone else is thinking. I think you would be better to not think and consider who has something to gain if you were back out in the open and what their endgame might be. A very smart man said to me once that you would not ever be defeated by someone smarter than you, but by someone that you couldn't understand because they were nowhere near as smart as you."

Michael looked serious as well and said, "Who would that be?"

Jay looked at Michael. "Never knew his name, but he knew you and talked highly of you. Appeared to know your family. Strange guy, met in a bar in Austin. He knew me as well and I never said a word, he just asked if I had seen you. I said I had no idea who you were. He talked for a short time, finished a Scotch and left. I asked about him to a controller later, they said he is a ghost and only took on charity cases."

"Seems we have something in common," Michael said, "but I have no clue who it would be. Wish you would have called me and told me."

"Told you what?" Jay mocked. "That some strange guy appeared and disappeared in a bar asking about you? I have always thought I may have been drunk at the time. It was before you found Janet for me, when things were really bad from time to time."

"I didn't find Janet," Michael laughed. "You did. I just happened to be there at that stupid bar in West Virginia egging you on."

"Well, with you," Jay broke in, "I never would have had the gumption to talk to her."

"Whatever," Michael said.

"Asshole," Jay returned. "So what now?"

"I am running a scan on the video, trying to find the place in the window," Michael said. "It will take some time, but the server I am on is pretty fast and should get us something eventually."

"Eventual Lee," Jay laughed. "Bruce Lee's brother?"

"Doofus," Michael said dryly. "Get a grip."

"What would you like me to grip?" Jay chuckled.

"Would you stop?" Michael said.

The plane continued to Portland as Michael looked back at his screen, willing it to find answers soon, knowing he might not like them.

Chapter 39 – Interception

Barbara came away from the cockpit and walked directly to Alex, which wasn't hard considering the plane wasn't very big.

"Master Sergeant," she said, "Satcom has locked onto the plane. We have a filed flight plan for Tokyo via Portland, Oregon. Estimates put them at Portland within two hours. Best speed puts us there in just under four hours. Should we have the plane detained in Portland?"

Alex considered his move. If he played it too early he may not know what was really going on, one of the general's goals. If they attempted to detain Masterson, it could be bad, either for him or for the forces used to detain him. If he did little or nothing, it could be as bad.

Alex looked thoughtful, then spoke, "Get a message to the airport, have them delay, but not detain. If we can get there, we will interact. For some reason he let me go once, I am not sure of his intentions and neither is the general. If we are not there, they are to proceed. Buy as much time as possible, but do not engage. Have Drake kick this thing in the guts, get as much out of her as he can. If we can contain this on U.S. soil without a fight, it will be better."

Alex thought for a second. "Jim, when we get there, I need some leeway, that is if we make it in time. I will go in alone and attempt to direct Masterson to a neutral location on the ground and maybe we can sort this out. You and Rachel find us a place that will be secure; barracks, a hangar, something."

Jim was smiling. "Leeway?" he laughed. "Sure, okay. Sounds like pure silliness, but I will go along for now."

Jim and Rachel moved to the seats next to each other and began working on a computer. It was apparent they could work well together quickly and they were looking at maps on a small screen deciding tactical advantages of each location.

"Ronnie," Alex stated.

"Sir," Ronnie almost jumped and stood to attention.

"Ronnie, first stop that shit. You have got to get a little looser. I need constant updates on our ETA and a check on whatever weapons we have on the plane. Work with Barbara for both and make this happen. I need a report on our full readiness in thirty minutes."

"Yes sir," Ronnie said, and walked to the front of the cabin and began talking to Barbara. He pointed and said a few things and she turned and looked at Alex with a light smirk, then began giving Ronnie information followed by leading him to the aft of the plane through the storage door. Alex was certain there were weapons in the back and of course they had theirs, but he didn't know the extent of the plane, nor how fully equipped it was and needed all of his assets available.

Picking up his sat phone, he called the general.

The phone came online quickly and no voice was in between on the number he had been given, just a straight shot to the general.

"Sir, I have information."

"Spit it out boy. I haven't got all day," the general fired back.

"Sir, we are sure they are heading to Tokyo via Portland. We will intercept there. I have asked the airport to delay, but not detain to avoid civilian interaction," Alex said hurriedly.

"Good thinking boy," the general praised. "What else?"

"We are prepping for a discussion. I am hoping we can figure this out with no more deaths," Alex reported.

"Listen up," the general said in a serious tone. "If it comes to it, you need to take him down quick and easy. Set the little prick, Jim, up to snipe the fucker if necessary, but don't let him get the drop on you again. There is just too much at stake."

"Yes sir," Alex stated.

"That it?" the general questioned.

"Yes sir," Alex stated and the phone went dead.

He thought of Masterson and how easily he took down both he and his team. This time would be different. He felt sorry for the young man, but knew his team would be ready.

Chapter 40 – Redirection

Portland, Oregon sported three airports and two of them were capable of landing this heavy plane. Jay and Michael had discussed the possibility they could be tracked and had also evaded such issues before, always seeming to stay one step ahead of everyone. Normally Michael would use commercial flights, but that took time and required even more effort to set up weapons and necessary equipment wherever he needed to be. In this case, getting to Japan was the easy part and they doubted there would be much problem there. Getting anywhere else, like, say North Korea, would be a challenge they would have to determine a course of action to complete later.

Jay reached into an overhead box and flipped off a switch, which turned off their transponder. He then got on his radio and transmitted, "Hillsboro Tower, this is GYZa55 Heavy, requesting permission to land."

As Jay used one radio, Michael used a second to talk to the Portland tower. "Portland Tower, this is GYZa55 Heavy. We are having an issue with our transponder and are circling for a moment while the engineer checks it out."

The Hillsboro tower answered Jay quickly, "GYZa55 Heavy, suggest divert to Portland International."

Jay replied as quickly. "Hillsboro Tower. I am running on fumes and there is always a line there. Request permission to land at Hillsboro."

As is usual, it came down to money. A full set of tanks for the big plane would mean a lot of cash for the smaller airport and someone would look good on paper. Jay and Michael just hoped they would bite.

"GYZa55 Heavy, clear to land on Runway 1," came the Hillsboro tower voice.

With practiced ease, Jay set the flaps and speed and the plane appeared to float like a feather to the ground. Michael was always amazed at how in tune Jay was with the plane and could make such a beast of a machine seem to be as tame as a hang glider. In a matter of minutes, the plane touched down and came to stop at the end of the runway.

Jay requested taxi information and was moving immediately to a large set of hangars where he powered down the engines and got out to wait for the fuel truck.

Michael again got on the radio. "Portland Tower, this is GYZa55 Heavy. We are still circling at 15,000 while the engineer checks electricals."

"GYZa55 Heavy," came the reply, "please key your mic so we can gain a radio fix."

Michael remained silent as the fuel truck drove up to the plane and Jay began doing what he did best, building relationships with strange people.

Jay laughed. "Yeah, I got drunk in Scotland one weekend and when I came back my arm was clean, but I had this damn tattoo on the plane."

Michael could see the gauges going up as fuel was pumped into the plane and was hopeful the ruse would work for long enough for them to get on their way. He knew they would probably have company somewhere, but wanted to control the meeting.

Below, Jay was telling a joke about the first time he wore a kilt in Scotland and giving the men advice on being really careful in front of nuns in the wind. The men were rolling with laughter as the fuel continued to flow.

"GYZa55 Heavy," came a voice, "this is Portland Tower. Please key your mic to allow radio tracking." Michael keyed the mic once, knowing the tower would see the distance and think the plane was somewhere over Hillsboro, but knowing they would not have time for a three-dimensional lock.

The gauges in the plane appeared full, so Michael began doing pre-flight checks to ensure it would be ready when Jay came back into the cockpit.

Looking down he saw the large lines were being removed by the fuel crew and Jay was reaching into a bag and giving the men a bottle of Johnnie Walker Blue. "Don't chug this boys. This is a fine sipping Scotch and made for real men."

The men laughed and thanked Jay as he signed the last bits of paperwork for the fuel bill. Then they got in the truck and drove off to the fuel depot while Jay sealed the plane back up.

Michael began spinning up the huge turboprop engines as Jay got into the cockpit.

"Jay put on his headset and called the Hillsboro tower. "This is GYZa55 Heavy, requesting permission for takeoff."

"GYZa55 Heavy, you are clear for takeoff on Runway 1," came the quick reply. "Stop by anytime," came the rather informal reply.

Jay taxied to the runway and powered up all four engines and was soon back in the air. The whole exchange had been less than thirty minutes.

Michael keyed his mic one more time. "Portland Tower, this is GYZa55 Heavy, still circling. Will make one more pass then come in."

"GYZa55 Heavy confirmed, one more pass," came the reply.

Jay smiled at Michael as they headed to the coast and the anonymity of the Pacific Ocean.

Chapter 41 – Irritation

"What the fuck do you mean you lost them," the general snarled. "I gave you a fucking speedster of a jet and a crack crew. You said you knew where they were going and you lost them?"

"Yes sir," Alex started. "They apparently set down at the smaller Portland airport while informing the larger Portland airport they were having issues. With air traffic controllers as overworked as they are, they managed to sneak in and out of the smaller airport fully fueled and were gone quickly."

"I don't believe this shit, boy," the general shot back. "I think you were just too busy trying to look good in that damn plane that he slipped by you. Not acceptable."

Drake piped in to the conversation. "Sir, I think they had this well planned. It was far too rehearsed and no one could have caught it."

"You think?" the general nearly screamed thorough the radio. "I don't pay you to fucking think. I pay you to fly the damn plane and handle things I can't deal with. Stop fucking thinking and catch this guy."

Ronnie cringed in the corner and Rachel rolled her eyes at the general's brusqueness. Jim just smiled and made semi obscene gestures with his hands every time he talked.

Alex was stoic in his response. "General, this is just a report. We will intercept and have a longer range and faster speed. We are reasonably sure where they are going and will use Satcom to get the job done and find out your answers. We are in route now and will advise as we progress. This was a setback, but you didn't expect this to be any easier than I did. We are not dealing with farmer Ted; we are dealing with someone who has been around the block a few times."

Not beaten from his tongue lashing a moment ago, Drake opened up again. "We also know that his pilot, McCloud, is a skilled pilot in his own right and has gotten around more than most pilots ever will. It is doubtful we would have been able to stop them in one place, even if we had locked down the airports. I am guessing they had pre-intel on what we set up and would have landed at a Sunoco and refueled if we had made it too tough. We are more likely to slow them down on foreign ground where other officials will be involved and not domestically where Jay's familiarity with the system will get him farther than we can predict."

The general was silent for a moment then spoke. "Alex, we still have not found the spook and we are having issues determining who he was beyond a certain point. I will let you know what these computer geeks find as they keep digging."

"Yes sir," Alex said. "Anything else sir?"

"Yeah," the general spat. "We went over your missile site. You were right. It was our missiles that hit your transports. Problem is, we have no launches detected and apparently no missing ordinance. It seems these are fucking ghost missiles and fly around killing people for the fuck of it. I am betting these little computer fucks are going to ask for a raise after I have them dig us out of this bullshit."

"Yes sir," Alex said. "I am sure they are doing their jobs well."

At the last comment, Jim spun Rachel around and started acting as though he were kissing her bottom as Ronnie, Rachel and Barbara covered their mouths to keep from laughing.

"The little shits better be doing their jobs well or I will kick their fucking asses all the way up to that damn plane you are on," the general almost seethed.

"Yes sir," Alex said. "Anything else?"

"Just get this asshole so we can figure this shit out," the general said in a more civilized tone. "And sergeant…"

"Sir," Alex said.

"Tell that little shit next to you this is a video phone and the next time I want to watch him kiss someone's ass, I will order it from the hotel channel." The general laughed then the line went dead.

Jim laughed so hard he could not see straight while Rachel, Ronnie and Barbara were mortified. Jim looked to the girls and noticed Barbara was chewing gum. He put his hand in front of her mouth and said, "Spit."

Barbara looked meekly and spit the gum out in Jim's hand. Jim went to the small conference phone with the small camera and spread the gum out on the lens.

"That takes care of that," he said, then laughed again.

"Terry," Alex broke in, "can we find them?"

"With their transponder off, probably not, but we will watch closely and at minimum beat them to Tokyo, if that is where they really want to be," Terry stated.

"Let's make this happen," Alex said, as he considered the general's words. "We keep getting questions, but we need answers."

Chapter 42 – Inclination

A flight over the Pacific Ocean is about as exciting as driving through Ohio, or Indiana for that matter. Occasionally there is something to see, but not very often. Michael's computer continued churning and comparing landscapes and items in the picture and found nothing of use except that it was similar to a painting done by an obscure French painter some fifty years previous. All of his phone calls had been a bust, with old contacts having no information on anything about Karen or her plight. It was shortly after they left Portland that Michael said they would go on as he had intended.

The waves below the big plane looked like lines etched on a blue green canvas, with no movement easily discernable from 25,000 feet and they were barely an hour out to sea.

Jay leaned back on the pilot's chair as the autopilot kept them level and on a GPS locked heading, while Michael read on his tablet about the newest weapons on the market and the trends in American gun control.

Michael had no issues with the government, simply because he felt he operated outside of the government. At one time he felt no one should be armed, because it made his job a lot easier. An unarmed sheep means cutlets for dinner. Having stopped doing what he did, Michael felt differently now because of people, mostly Abby, not having a right to protect themselves. It made no sense.

Being a skilled debater, Michael could argue either side and had done so once in college, making a mockery of the normal debates by debating gun control against himself. He did it so effectively that even the outraged professor was eventually applauding at the creative sides that Michael seemed to instantly pull out and relay to himself.

It was amazing to Michael how foolish both sides were. It was very telling to him how people could be so easily swayed by political jargon. On one side, the conservatives believing no control is a good thing, perfectly stupid or not, while on the other the liberals believing that a criminal would be inclined to follow a law, which was also perfectly stupid. In the end, only the law abiding honest people of the country were hurt either way, by either restricting their rights or reinforcing their need for a government who did all but wipe their bottoms.

Michael eventually had to turn off the tablet as the propaganda from both sides was mostly lies and silliness anyway.

"So," Michael started, "how are you and Janet doing?"

Jay smiled, true seriousness on his mind for once. "Have I told you how happy I am that you helped us get together?" I mean, it is one thing to find someone to be with. The Lord knows I did that with my first wife. To find someone who is as passionate about life as I am, though and, and this is a big and, and...who will put up with my utter nonsense, strange work ethic and even stranger friends is simply impossible. But it works for us."

At that last part Michael had crinkled his nose up wondering if he was a "strange friend" and Jay had smiled as he said it.

"You know Michael, of all the people I know, you are not the strangest. Not even close," Jay stated before Michael could say a word. "I know what you have done and some of it is scary, but I have seen the other side of you. When your walls come down you are one of the nicest people I have ever met. How you are with Abby is the stuff most people dream of in their lives. I knew a man and woman once and everyone they knew adored them. They thought that man and woman had the most perfect relationship in the world, but then one day they found out she cheated on him. He was a prince to her and it broke his heart. In the end they divorced and went their separate ways and everyone was shocked. I wasn't, because you could tell. I know you would have been able to tell also since you are able to read people like cheap novels. There was just something missing and there should never be anything missing. For you and Abby, there is nothing missing. You adore her and worship the ground she walks on. She adores you even more and I think she would be here with us, right now, life on the line, if you would let her."

"I bet she would," said Michael with a sly look. "She is aware of everything and a damn good shot. I could think of a lot of worse people to have by my side."

"Do you see it?" Jay continued. "She would walk into hell for you. I know so many people that never get that chance or something messes it up." Jay smiled. "Funny story. You will not believe it. I was in a bar in Scotland a few years ago..."

Michael broke in with a gasp, "You in a bar, oh my God."

"Shut up," Jay took back control. "I am serious. I was in a bar and this giant man came in and sat next to me. Normally I get worked up by this, but well, this guy was different. He looked like a mountain and was vaguely familiar, but when he started talking it was apparent he was in a more than somber mood."

"Somber in a bar," Michael broke in again.

"Shhhhh," Jay said, "So he comes in and sits next to me, looks at the bartender and orders a whole bottle of twenty-year Scotch. He throws money on the bar and starts pouring shots and starts telling me about how he had lost his love and never knew anyone like her. Now this was an older guy, so I got into the conversation and asked if he had ever been married. He took a drink and looked at me and told me once, to a crazy bitch that sucked the life right out of him. The whole experience made him sell everything and start doing odd jobs around the world. When he said "odd jobs", I knew what he meant. So anyway, he tells me he met a woman once and they were perfect for each other, but she was married and he was doing odd jobs, so he didn't stick around. He said he felt like a fool leaving her, but even though she said she loved him, she could not love him and all that shit. It was reading like a bad play until he started pouring me shots too and we downed that bottle in silence, then another. While on the third I finally asked this mountainous man why he was thinking about it now." Jay paused for a moment.

"...and," Michael said.

Jay sat silently. A tear welled up and he choked it down, then pulled himself together. "And he looked me straight in the eye and said, 'You know, there are lots of chances in life, we take some that give us pure prosperity and some bring us the pain that will hurt till the end of time. It is the chances we give up on that hurt the most, because you know how it could have been, if you would have just believed in "what if?". The woman I loved so much and never knew and the woman who loved me, who didn't know me, died, and with it any chance of knowing how amazing life could be. If there is a heaven I know I deserve it, for this most assuredly is hell.' So I was a little stunned and tried to get up and obviously I had just downed over a liter of Scotch myself, so I didn't get far, like about two steps when the world started spinning." Jay's voice quickened, "And here is one thing that is unbelievable. He got up and grabbed me and picked me up like I was nothing and set me down at a booth in the bar. He wasn't drunk or didn't seem drunk at all. Then he sat down for a second and said to me, "Find love, Jay and make it the most important thing in your life, with your love never ever being second. Then he got up and left. So I tried to get up and was spinning like an overactive merry-go-round. I finally stood and he was gone."

"So?" Michael said.

"So," Jay broke in again, "so I never told him my name. I think he was my guardian Scotch angel." Jay smiled. "It was a year later you introduced me to Jane, and ever since his words echo in my head. She is always first. Always."

"Nice story," Michael said. "Reminds me of the old one about two drunks walking into a bar."

Jay frowned a little. "Damnit Michael, what you have is something most people never get to know. I know a little about your story and your mom and dad, but don't take this lightly. Believe you and Abby are the most important thing in the world. Live it, love it."

Michael paused with an almost sad look on his face. "I never forget Jay, not even for a moment. I could have been that man. Instead my mother taught me the right way and my father showed me it was right. I am easily two sides of a coin, amazed by life and love, but inclined to do what I must do. I am a winner because I will always do what I have to do."

Jay smiled. "Nice talk."

They paused for a moment as both of them scanned the vastness of the ocean below, at the same time considering the vastness of their lives and how random it was to find someone so precious.

In front of Michael, his computer started blinking, waiting silently for him to pay attention.

Chapter 43 – Exertion

Abby was the perfect hostess. She made sure Madison was comfortable and Janet was kept occupied. Where it seemed Madison would be happy to be a lump on a rock, Janet was full of energy and fifteen years older than Madison.

The first part of the day had been easy, working on the house and getting it ready for an almost normal life. Well, as normal as any life could be with Michael. The three had talked about normal things; the home, family and the future. Madison wasn't very interesting and almost as positive as a black storm cloud, but Janet was upbeat and positive about everything in life, especially about Jay.

Both Janet and Abby tried to get Madison out of her morbid outlook of the world, but all she could do was say how cheated she had been in life by her parents, how bad it was living around her parents, how her parents had tried to guide her every thought and how she had given up Michael because of her parents.

Janet was adamant that Madison would find someone and they would be more exciting than Michael, but that only made it worse as the house they sat in was due to Michael's exceptional planning and the way it was built was a testament to his love for Abby.

Finally, Abby had enough. She looked at Madison and said in a sickeningly sweet voice, "You have no one to blame but yourself. God, I can't believe how much I revered you when we were in school. You had Michael and it was obvious he loved you, but you never really let him, did you? You were so caught up in what your parents wanted that you didn't make a decision for yourself. You didn't love him enough to stay, love him enough to explain, love him enough to find your way back, and in the end, he was frustrated and upset because of your lack of forethought. You may as well have said the devil made you do it or you had a sign from heaven, because nothing you have said was worth saying. If you loved him, you would have found a way. If you didn't you should have. He deserved for you to sit down and talk it through, not pawn it off on some nebulous shit. I hope when you do find someone, and in this world I am sure you will, that you treat them as they deserve to be treated and not like some used Kleenex you can flush down the toilet at will."

Madison's eyes were as wide as the saucers on an English tabletop at tea, as were Janet's.

"Damnit," Abby said, "can you just get your head out of your ass and realize that he loved you. That was a gift. I know every day with him could be my last, so I never let an opportunity pass to be with him, to love him and to damn well make sure he knows it."

Abby put her head down for a second, waving her hand. "So listen little girl. You need to get your shit together. My life could be at an end right now because my love, the person I want to be with always, is out doing something for you. You need to be thankful for that. Instead of being a whiney little brat, step up and do something worthwhile. If you can't, I have two simple words for you; fuck and you."

Abby put her hands up as the two women kept staring and walked to the spiral staircase and below to the gym.

She walked to the brand new heavy bag on the side of the room and felt the smooth leather with her hands. The logo of the bag was even softer and she relaxed as she reached above the bag, pulling down the bag gloves and slipping them on her hands.

Abby was worried. She knew the risks; she always knew the risks. He was Michael. Even after he stopped, his playfulness in the mountains with all kinds of mountainfolk in Kentucky, his silly escapades and even the immediate response he had for intruders just a day ago put him in harm's way often. It was as if he courted the gods and always came out ahead, but was always on the edge of oblivion. Abby wished Madison had never found them and he would not be going this new direction.

Abby began punching the bag. It was slow for her and she was careful not to twist or bend her wrist. Michael had taught her that; he had taught her so much.

She began punching faster and working herself into a rhythm. It was slow going and Michael had taught her to trigger her punches with each hand by slow taps followed by a hard punch. The combination was usually effective with "noobs", Michael said as real fighters could see it coming. It did make for a good workout though.

Abby considered their life together all the wonderful things they had shared. The passion they had for each other, those times when Michael actually needed her as he was awash with feelings about his mother, the things he should have said and done.

Abby knew Michael's dark secret about his father and the lack of guilt he felt. She knew those led to his "miss" and his move away from being a silent specter of death and instead helping people, even when they didn't know it.

Her thoughts drifted as she punched the bag until a hand was on her shoulder. She swung around fast, grabbing the hand and bringing it forward as Michael had taught her, the body falling straight to the mat as she lowered herself to deliver a punch and saw Madison looking up at her.

Madison's eyes were red with tears and wide with more than a little fear.

Abby stood up. "I'm sorry," she said. "You shouldn't sneak up on people like that."

Madison sat and pulled her legs in close to her, then put her arms around her legs and rested her chin on them.

"No, Abby," she said. "I'm sorry. I have been a real self-centered ass and no one has ever said it like you did."

"Yes, you have," Abby said as she resumed punching the bag. "It's about time you saw it for yourself." Abby switched and began alternating punches and quick kicks to the bag and was pounding it hard when Madison spoke.

"I really am sorry, Abby. Not just to Michael, but to you. You were always so nice to me and I never appreciated you either." Madison almost wept again.

Abby hit the bag one more time and stopped. She held the bag for a moment, pausing, considering, thinking about all the things that had run through her mind. "I need to live by my rules too, Madison," she said as she put the bag gloves on top of the heavy bag.

Abby reached out a hand to Madison. Madison slowly looked up, reached out her hand and leaning back a little first, pulled herself up. Abby gave her a hug and said, "Forgiven."

"Abby, I don't deserve you or Michael, but thank you," Madison choked out.

"Damn right," Abby said as she stepped back, "but you did deserve the sweat. Let's get ourselves together and head into town. We can get some groceries and do a little shopping. I don't expect much. If Michael picked this place I am sure it is small, but it should be fun exploring."

Madison wiped the sweat from herself as she listened to Abby. "Yeah, okay. I don't have much in the way of clothes, but it will be fun."

"Did I hear someone say shopping?" Janet said from the stairs. "Let's get this show on the road," she said and Madison and Abby headed up for a different kind of adventure.

Chapter 44 – Detection

"I think we have them," stated Terry excitedly to Alex and the group lounging in the back of the Gulfstream. "We have a target 150 miles in front of us with no transponder. We have confirmation it matches the size of our target, but no clear picture as of yet."

Alex perked up immediately. "How long will it take us to intercept?" he asked excitedly.

"We should be over them in about twenty minutes, but we are having a hard time tracking them consistently without the transponder." Terry stated.

"How long until we have a visual?" Jim asked.

"It will be hard to guess," Terry said. "There is some cloud cover and we are guessing at their altitude."

Jim looked at Alex. "If this guy is as good as you say, we should slow down and shadow, let him play his hand. We have nothing we can do up here and I doubt they know we are following them. There could be three or four people on the plane or there could be thirty. I am not sure you want them walking out of the plane somewhere, fully aware of our intentions."

Alex nodded, "Terry, slow us down and let's see where this goes. We will assume this is our target and hopefully we are not on a wild goose chase."

Terry nodded and walked back to the cockpit.

Jim looked and started talking to Alex while Rachel came closer to both of them. "By the way, "boss", what are our intentions? You said this guy took you down pretty quickly. If there are a dozen of them in there, we will not be able to make a dent with the four of us. If there are one or two, they have the element of knowing where they are going and what they are doing and we have virtually no idea of what is really going on.

Are we going to ask them to dance? Are we going to try to follow someone who can disappear? Or fight someone who can neutralize four soldiers, including you, like most people sling snot off their fingers?"

At the last metaphor, Rachel made a crunched up face and whispered "ewww."

"Sorry," Jim continued, "but we all need to know what is going to happen now that we have some clue of a target. You are leading this little shindig and I will follow along, but I didn't get signed up by someone who cusses more than George Carlin only to get killed because we don't have a plan."

"Understood," Alex said. "Honestly, I didn't expect to catch up this fast, but I still think he doesn't want to kill anymore. I am not sure why, but as easily and ruthlessly as he killed the man he questioned, I don't think we are in danger from him. I am more worried about the unknown that killed my men."

"Same difference," Jim said. "Not trying to be an asshole."

Rachel cut in, "Yes you are, it seems to come naturally."

"Okay," Jim broke back in, "maybe I am being an asshole, but I want to be a living asshole."

"Same here," said Rachel. "Well, I want to be a living person, not an asshole. Well, you know what I mean."

"Me too," said Ronnie from the back. "At least I think me too."

"Well then," Alex stated, "it is easy. I am not going to put any of you in danger. So when we set down, I am going to walk onto that plane and ask him just what the hell is going on."

"That's your plan?" Jim said. "Hate to say it, but that is stupid and I didn't get any Frequent Flyer Miles for riding in this rig. So I really don't want you dead and me heading home in this thing."

Alex laughed. "Well, I think I will be a little more prepared than just doing it alone. I am just not going to put you in danger. We need to get him on the ground where we have the distance advantage."

Jim laughed this time. "You know this is like trying to catch a piranha with your teeth using your tongue as bait, don't you?

"Maybe so, but I have you," Alex said. "Terry, can we get blueprints of Tokyo and all the airports close. Let's work out a hangar for ground control to send them to so we can control the outcome more effectively. You did our weapons check; can we cover effectively? Rachel, you are good at close range, how about at a distance?"

Jim smiled, "This is more like it. See, you just need to keep pushing."

Alex smiled again, "I guess so."

The team began putting a plan together, a plan they hoped would keep them all alive.

Chapter 45 – Perfection

Madison was appalled. She had agreed to go into "town" with Janet and Abby, but she wasn't sure she agreed to be on a lost episode of Green Acres. Dubois, Wyoming was a thriving metropolis of about 1,000 people normally and was supported by a lot of tourists trying to get "back into nature".

When they drove through the town, Madison was a little disturbed there were no malls, no big stores and that the first store they passed was a Family Dollar. To her it didn't get better as she sat in the back seat looking out the window. Janet and Abby, on the other hand, were excited by every store they passed, from the obvious Dubois Super Foods to the several little curiosity shops and cafes.

Madison thought the two were going to explode with excitement when they saw a candy and small general store, but she was really scared when they stopped and dragged her along to go in.

The small coffee shop, Kathy's Coffee, was first on their list as Abby just had to have something from around there and Janet just wanted coffee. Janet had said she needed a coffee fix since they were at the house and when they walked in the store, the smells were overpowering.

It is amazing how so many people just don't stop and smell the coffee. In this case, though, that's just what Janet did as she just breathed in the coffee smell and felt like she was in heaven. Madison was a little interested by this, but she was a bit taken back that she didn't have Starbucks and a croissant.

"Yummy," Abby said looking at a menu.

"You are kidding," Madison said quietly.

A woman walked up to them and said, "Howdy, my name's Kathy. How can I help you?"

Abby took point as usual, "Howdy back. How about two black coffees, you pick, and a green tea latte for the sourpuss in the back."

"Hey!!" Madison said.

"Would you like anything else?" the woman asked.

"Abby, look at this," Janet said as she eyed a giant cookie. The cookie was bigger than anything you could get at a Subway or McDonalds and had huge chocolate chunks in it that stood out like boulders on the moon.

"And three of those cookies," Abby said.

Abby paid quickly and the girls sat down at a small table and waited for their order. It was surprising how quickly it came out and Janet became a coffee drinking machine as she downed the cup in just a few minutes and went for a refill.

Abby noticed a huge man walk in and walk to the counter. His arms rippled as he walked and his shadowy grey hair was cut short and parted to the side. His features were as though they were cut from marble and she thought he was handsome for an older man, if a little mysterious, but it was his eyes that caught Abby's attention. Their hazel color seemed to shimmer as he walked and she swore they looked blue for a moment, only to look green, then brown, based completely on where he stood. Abby realized she was staring when Madison poked her in the side.

"What?" Abby said.

"Getting an eyeful?" Madison smiled.

"No," Abby said, "I mean, did you see his eyes?"

"No, I saw the weird necklace," Madison returned.

Abby looked back and noticed the necklace around the man's neck, from a golden chain hung what looked like a clump of metal, but it ended in a point.

"Chai again, hon?" Kathy said from behind the counter.

"Yes, ma'am." The man spoke in a soft, but strangely powerful deep voice.

"Coming right up," Kathy said as she brought out the girls' order.

"You gals need anything else?" she asked as she set everything down on a table.

"Nope," Abby said. "Thank you, though."

"It's my job," said Kathy, and walked back to the counter as the other young lady finished making the Chai.

"Thank you, ma'am," the giant said as he took the tea and left a bill on the counter. "Please keep the change."

"Always do," said Kathy. "Sure you aren't up for a date, I have a friend..."

"I am sure you do," the man said. "Every time I am in here you have a friend." He smiled and his smile was infectious. "Have an amazing day," he said as he walked out the door.

Abby, Madison and Janet turned and watched through the window as he left. As he got into his truck, they saw the two huge black dogs sitting in the back tracking his every move.

Madison laughed and said, "woof" and as she did the two dogs turned and looked straight at her, making the small group feel very uneasy for a moment. The man started the large F350 and drove off, with the dogs watching them until they were no longer in sight.

"Weird," Abby said.

"Scary," Madison said.

Kathy walked up and looked at them. "Yeah, he is different, but he is a good customer and those dogs of his, wow. Some of the people here think they are wolves, but no one has asked. He comes into town and gets a tea from time to time and everyone remembers him. How is everything?"

Abby gleamed. "This cookie is perfection and the coffee is just right."

Janet looked at Kathy. "The coffee is great, one more cup please?" she said.

"Thank you," Kathy nodded at Abby. "Coming right up," Kathy said to Janet and walked back to the counter.

"Where do we start?" Madison said. "Should we drive to a real city?"

Abby looked at Madison and smiled. "You would think you could adapt with all the stuff you have been through. No, we will make do. Finish your tea and let's get moving. We will get what we can find for clothes, then grab groceries and head home. If you need anything else, we can probably get it at the Dollar General or one of the general stores. We can get anything here; we may just have to ask around."

"Kathy," Janet said to the woman who was cleaning up in the mid-day lull, "where can we get a few outfits around here?"

"Well, you should be able to get something down at Welty's. It is a bit touristy, but they will do ya right. There is also a thrift shop and there may be some yard sales around. Just keep your eyes peeled."

"Thanks," Janet said.

The three girls finished their cookies quickly as Madison seemed to brood in the corner about the idea of having to go to a yard sale as a primary source of clothes.

As they stood and cleaned up their small table Abby said, "Thanks!" and Kathy nodded and smiled.

Abby, Madison, and Janet walked out of the coffee shop and got into the Suburban. As they drove the short distance to the General Store, they didn't see the black Ford Focus fall in behind them like a silent shark, circling its prey.

Vengeful Son

Chapter 46 – Bisection

Michael was down in the Suburban checking over his gear when he heard Jay over the intercom.

"Michael, you need to see this," came the echoing voice.

Michael closed up the car and headed back up the steps to the cockpit. As he walked in he asked Jay, "What's up?"

"We appear to have a shadow," Jay said.

"Where?" Michael sat down in the co-pilot's chair.

"About twenty miles behind us and high, but matching our speed and course. I don't think they know we are tracking them, they are not being too stealthy about it," Jay said.

"Can you ID the plane from here?" Michael asked.

"No, not really, but it came up on us fast. I doubt we can outrun it. Ideas?" Jay said.

Michael considered for a moment and looked at the onboard radar screen. "You still have the transponder off?"

"Yep. I bet that's how they found us. If they were tracking us via sat and saw no transponder, we probably stood out. That's my fault." Jay stated.

"Can you still clone transponders?" Michael asked.

"Well, it is against the…," Jay started.

"So is turning it off, so can you still clone them or not?" Michael said gruffly.

"Of course," Jay said. "Not going to do us much…"

"Sure it is." Michael pointed to the Radar screen. "Let's get our little tail to playout his hand. Gear this thing up and get as close as you can, then clone on the pass and spin. Let's see who he follows."

"Nice idea," Jay smiled. "Bet they think we are blind," Jay said, as he pulled back on the yoke and turned heading towards a blip on the radar.

Michael looked at him, "Close as you dare."

Jay laughed, "Close as you dare? Who talks like that?"

Michael smiled as the plane grumbled, "How far?"

"Two miles or so," Jay said, as they continued to climb.

"Are you ready?" Michael asked. "You only have a few seconds."

"Yep," Jay said, flipping a switch center console. A light flashed red under the switch as they saw the plane's tail and came up on it fast.

"You will need to brake as you break off so we seem to be at the same speed," Michael said.

Jay looked at Michael, "Who has done this more?"

Michael smiled as the light under the switch turned green. Jay came up under the plane in front of them, a large passenger jet, then washed slowly in front and left of it. The jet's pilot, seeing the other plane, veered right to avoid the overly close plane and the potential wash from that plane creating a split. Jay hit the now flashing green button and bisected an invisible line between them, throttling back as he did so, nearly matching the speed of the other plane.

He then slowly started vectoring back towards Tokyo just as the other plane had, while slowly veering away as well.

It would take a few minutes to see if their shadow took the bait and chose one of them.

Michael looked at Jay. "We may need a plan B to avoid talking to our tail too soon."

Jay laughed. "I think I can deal with that", and started descending towards the ocean.

Michael's laptop started beeping wildly where it sat to the right of the co-pilot's chair.

"What now?" Michael said loudly.

Michael looked at the computer and studied it intently as Jay kept descending towards the ocean. Michael looked up for a moment and saw the blue green waters were now slowly rising to meet them, making waves and eddies more visible.

"Jay," Michael asked, "How much fuel do we have?"

"Plenty to get to Japan," Jay replied.

"How about to Texas?" Michael countered.

"Texas," Jay laughed. "A lot of good bars in Texas. What the heck would we do there, though? Madison's mom leave a clue?"

"Well, can we make it?" Michael asked again.

"No issue and if we can't, we have access to all sorts of airports along the way," Jay replied. "We will have to turn the transponder back on as we come in or we might get shot at. So they will know something is there, but I can use a stored key if you want."

"No," Michael said." Let's see where this takes us. It looked like the video was shot outside of San Antonio, Texas. A lot of this may well be a ruse. Apparently I didn't see this thing flashing at me earlier and we have wasted some time, but maybe it will set our course without a tail now. This is interesting and it makes me wonder if the North Koreans at the house were involved or trying to find Madison to see what was really going on as well. I have a friend, well, an acquaintance in North Korea, I helped once and I am pretty sure he could fill us in, but I dare not get him involved at the moment. We will see where this takes us, but I would rather explore the pretty solid domestic possibility before taking on a country that we may not even need to go to. The point is, this video may be invalidating all the information Madison was fed by our government."

"You called that one," Jay laughed. "I bet we find some North Korean look alike there."

"Possibly," Michael said, "but I am not sure how this all fits together. Should be an interesting engagement. When we are done, we should write a book."

"Yeah, funny. You write a book, I am thinking, 'The man who shot damn near everyone,' by the man with no name." Jay giggled.

The sea was now close as Jay was flying at only a few hundred feet above the ocean below.

"Killing the transponder and heading south. I will turn it back on as we get close to LA and fly us up. Between the low altitude and no transponder, we are about to disappear," Jay said in a more serious tone.

"Thanks, Jay," Michael said, "I never tell you thank you enough."

"Sure you do," Jay said, "but you can buy me another Scotch sometime."

"I'm sure I can," Michael said. "I am sure I can."

Chapter 47 – Inflection

"You lost them?" Alex said with an incredulous tone that made the team cringe. "How in the hell could we have lost them?"

Terry broke in, "We didn't exactly lose them. We seem to have lost the original target."

"Wanna explain that to me?" Alex said.

"Uh-oh, someone is in trouble now," Jim said.

"Shut up," Rachel whispered to him.

Terry and Alex both looked at Jim and Rachel, then turned back to each other.

Terry started, "We now have two possible planes and we are not sure which the right one is. They are both ahead of us and if we converge on either one of them, we will tip the right one off. It appears they know we are back here and are looking for us to make a move."

"We still have eyes on both?" Alex said.

Terry nodded.

"Then follow at the same distance so we can stay in range of both," Alex said.

"Will do," Terry said.

Jim smiled, "I wish I had an Easy Button right now so I could slap it."

Rachel smirked, "I bet you would like easy."

Jim laughed.

"So what's the plan now?" Jim asked Alex.

"Find me a place we can pen him down," Alex said. "Get on it."

"Will do," Jim said and tapped Rachel on the shoulder. "Computer time again, let's get on it."

Alex sat down and began going over the list of items Barbara and Ronnie had identified. It appeared they had a small arsenal in the plane, hidden away in compartments in the back of the Gulfstream. He smiled as he came to the Barrett and knew that Jim would be in heaven with the massive weapon.

He looked over to the side and saw Ronnie had fallen asleep. They still had a quite a few hours to go and only a few hours to determine which plane had Michael in it.

Terry yelled to the back of the plane. "Alex!"

Alex ran back up to the cockpit, "What is it?"

"The south plane, it just dropped off the radar and the transponder went dark." Terry said hurriedly.

"Looks like we found which plane they were," Alex said, "but I am not quite sure of their game. Any ideas?"

"I will head to the last known and we will try to pick them up," Terry said.

"Let's get them," Alex said as he moved back to sit down.

"You do know how big the Pacific Ocean is, don't you?" Terry asked.

Terry Drake swung the plane south and increased speed to find a needle in a haystack.

Chapter 48 – Sedation

Madison, Abby and Janet were laughing at the shopping they had done. Initially Madison had been a stick in the mud with the thrift store idea and Abby's lack of any need for designer clothes, but when they got to the General Store, Madison was in her element and even got excited about boots.

Abby had to stop Madison in the middle of getting ready to pay as she had pulled out a credit card. Madison protested, but Abby pulled out a stack of crisp 100-dollar bills and said they needed to use cash. Michael had taught her that credit meant detection almost anywhere. Abby had also initially been a bit over the top watching for cameras everywhere, but in the town of Dubois, there just weren't that many to worry about.

With bags in hand, Abby, Madison and Janet headed to the big Suburban in the empty lot next to the General Store. The black Suburban was one of only a few cars in the lot and Abby noticed the Ford Focus sitting only a few cars away. The Focus had very dark windows and was unusually clean compared to the few other cars in the lot. As they approached the front of the Suburban, Abby was wary. As if in response to her caution, when two men came around the passenger side of the car, she loudly said, "Hello," alerting Janet and Madison to the oncoming people. A second later another man came around the driver's side of the Suburban and Abby knew this was going to be a problem.

Janet dropped her bags, as did Abby and looked towards the men. Madison stood dumbfounded and not certain of what was going on.

"You are going to need to come with us," the man on the driver's side said. "We really don't want to hurt you."

"I have read that book before," Abby said, while raising her hands up and taking a boxing stance, "and I think she wrote the book." Abby nodded towards Janet while not taking her eyes off of the man.

"Let's not make this any harder than it has to be, Abby." the man said.

Abby was dead cool and showed no reaction as the man came within a few feet. As he did, Abby feigned a punch with her left arm. The man shifted to avoid her punch, but Abby pivoted her weight quickly to her right leg and kicked the man in the side of the knee. "No, let's," she said, as he went down sideways to one knee.

Abby stepped back, but the man grabbed her foot and twisted it, making her fall face first in the dirt of the parking lot. She used her other foot to kick backwards into his face, forcing him to release his grip and get a mouthful of Wyoming soil.

While Abby backed off, Janet punched her attacker in the face twice and missed the third as he came forward into her. She had an issue with close quarters, so she simply stepped hard on his instep with her new cowboy boots fresh from the General Store. He screamed, but didn't let go, so Janet slammed her forehead into his chin and heard the crunch as she connected. If she had not broken his jaw, she had popped a tooth loose or something similar. The man let go and fell back holding his jaw.

Madison had not been much of an issue as her attacker simply had grabbed her when she dropped her bags. Struggle as she might, she didn't move or gain purchase.

The first man stood holding himself. "Not bad," he said and reached behind his back and pulled out a Glock 26. The 9mm was small, but would do the job. He pointed it at Abby and smirked. "This had to be easy," he smiled. Then he swung the gun to Janet as well. "Time to stop."

The second man moved to Janet and grabbed her from behind, holding her around her neck and chest.

"Damnit," Abby said, still seething with adrenaline.

Abby glanced to Madison and noticed the man holding her pulling out a syringe, with which he promptly injected Madison. As he did she yelped, then went limp.

The man laid her down surprisingly gently, then pulled out another syringe. Abby stepped back, but the man raised the gun towards her. "Ah, ah, ah," he said, as Abby stopped in her tracks.

She looked him in the eye with utter defiance, "No escape sweetheart. It would have been easier if you had just come with us."

The next few seconds were a blur that Abby and Janet would talk about forever. The gunman's arm was pulled down, with him in a blur of black fur, as a giant dog grabbed his hand and the associated gun in the equivalent of white razor blades. His hand was pinned by a set of teeth that looked capable of splitting not just his arm in half, but his entire body. The dog shook ever so slightly and the gun fell to the ground.

His partner holding Janet was gaping as a huge arm grabbed him from behind at his arms and both pulled his arms away from the woman, allowing her to be free, and lifted the man twelve inches off the ground.

With contemptuous ease, he threw the man to the ground and dared him to move with a look that would turn Medusa to stone.

The third man dropped the syringe and was reaching around to his back, but was suddenly thrown forward as a second giant black dog slammed down on him from behind. With his face in the ground, the dog's massive muzzle moved to his ear and growled ever so softly.

The third man shook like a leaf and slowly moved his hands out as they trembled like a jackhammer in a blender.

The first man looked up. "Call it off," he screamed, even though the dog barely held him.

The giant man said, "Shhhh," and his massive features relaxed a little. "If she doesn't like you she can snap your arm in half."

The man quieted, but still said, "You don't know who you are fucking with."

"Now, now," the giant man said again quietly. "I know exactly who I am, ahem, messing with, and I have files on all three of you. I also know about your parents, your friends, your neighbors," he nodded to the second man, "your affair and more than enough to wipe your bloodline off the face of the planet."

All three men looked a little less confident. "You best back off," the first man said a little less confidently, as the second man scrambled backwards a little, looking very confused.

"Vishnu, bring him over here." The giant black dog holding the first man's hand walked slowly to the giant, dragging the man along as he screamed in pain.

"I will not back off." The giant man leaned down and said, "You will get in your car and drive back to the airport, then out of here in your little plane or I will have her decide which part of you she wants to rip off. Then I will take some time to explore your family history."

The man still looked defiant as the giant made a pinch symbol with his hand where his fingers were apart; as he slowly moved them together the man squirmed and twisted in pain as the dog obviously was crushing his bone.

"All right, all right!" he said.

The giant man swung his two fingers apart and the dog let go of the man's arm, who quickly grabbed his wrist and babied it while backing himself away from the dog.

Vishnu walked to the giant man, turned and sat next to him on one side, dark eyes riveted to the man he had just walked away from. The man snapped his fingers and the second dog moved off the third man and went to the man's other side. The second man started to move and both dogs growled quietly.

"Leave the gun," the big man said.

The dogs narrowed their eyes and seemed to peer into the man's soul as their hackles rose. The second man shivered uncontrollably for a moment, then took the gun out and hurriedly and nervously dropped it to the ground.

"Thank you," the big man said softly as a butler would to their master as Janet scrambled over to Madison.

Abby moved to Madison as well, but kept her eyes on both the big man and the men who were watching and getting in the car. A small crowd had formed across the street and Abby knew the police would be here soon, with questions she wasn't sure how to answer.

The big man looked at her. "We need to get you out of here. I will take care of the police." He walked to Madison and bending down, put two huge hands under her and lifted her effortlessly. Janet opened the back door and the massive man who just saved them, almost brutally, laid Madison in the back seat with a gentleness that could only be described as caring.

The man then grabbed bags around the Suburban and took them to the back of the big vehicle. He opened the doors and filled the back cargo area as Abby tried to help.

"Who are you?" Abby asked, as Janet got into the front of the car and they closed the back doors.

"Alan," he said then paused for a moment. "Abby, you need to go. We will talk another time."

"Does everyone know me?" Abby said.

"Not everyone," he returned as he hurried her to the driver's door. "Now get out of here." He turned to the dogs, "Shiva! Vishnu!" and he pointed to the truck as the dogs ran over and jumped in to the open windows. Abby had not seen the truck, nor heard it, but it must have been there all the time.

"I'll see you again," he said. "Now stay in the house and no more shopping."

Abby drove off from the parking lot, wondering who this man was and what was going on that he would know her. She looked in the rearview mirror and watched the man as he dwindled in size at the same time the flashing lights of the police showed up.

Chapter 49 – Hydration

Jay swung the plane off the deck and brought it up to 25,000 feet. As he did he turned on the transponder again to ensure they would not be chased down by the great men of the United States Air Force.

"Los Angeles flight control, this is GYZa55 Heavy passing through your airspace. 25,000 feet at 120 relative," Jay said into his microphone as they came up on twenty-five miles from the coast.

"Roger GYZa55 Heavy," came the voice on the radio. "Proceed to 30,000 feet hold 120 relative."

"Roger Los Angeles flight control," Jay said.

Jay looked at Michael and smiled, "Walk in the park, eh?"

Michael laughed. "Yeah, a four hour walk Jay, that's a lot of airspace to walk through and we know we are being followed by someone."

Jay smiled. "We can deal with that here. They only thing I am having trouble dealing with is how sore my ass is getting."

Michael laughed. "You would think it is padded enough."

Jay frowned. "Really? I have been losing weight." Jay stayed almost serious for a moment until they both broke out laughing.

Michael shifted the conversation. "Jay, look at this." He flipped the computer around. "This set of trees and the tower in the background are 100% on the outskirts of San Antonio in an abandoned building. Based on my review, it seems to be the Good Samaritan Hospital that they have been trying to renovate."

"I know that place," said Jay. "I sent some money down to it a few years ago because I thought it was a good cause."

Michael looked at Jay, "Really?"

"Sure," Jay said. "I try to help some things some times and came across that one in a bar in Dallas and just had to do it."

"You in a bar?" Michael smiled.

"Hard to believe," Jay laughed.

"So anyway, this hospital is supposed to be abandoned, but I logged on to CPS energy and they are feeding it power. I also found that whoever is paying, isn't," Michael continued.

"Huh?" Jay questioned.

"Well, there is no bill to, no name, no nothing. It is almost like someone hacked the power on and have it trapped instead of billed," Michael continued.

"Yeah, I have seen that when I was at BG Energy years ago. They have it blocked when it is owned by the company. Never saw it on a non-company owned item," Jay said.

"Well, we have the where, or at least a 97.67 percent chance we have the where. I need the why, the how and the who now," Michael said.

"Well, at least we aren't heading to North Korea. I mean, that place can be a little out there sometimes," Jay said.

Michael nodded. "But that means North Korea was there for another reason. The man who told me they were from North Korea was not lying," Michael said. "I worked for North Korea years ago on one job. There was a general who had an aide trying to kill him. I tracked the aide for a few days and found where he was hiding. It was a watch and learn situation and eventually I verified he was planning to kill the general. I reported and the general told me to eliminate him," Michael said.

Jay was enthralled by the story, "And…"

Michael was nonchalant. "And I tracked him to his home, watched him through my scope eating dinner with his wife and children, watched him put his children to bed and kiss his wife goodnight and while she was getting into bed and he was drinking a cheap wine looking out the back window, I took everything he was and all that he would ever be," Michael paused. "It was quick and painless. He felt nothing and I had measured the round so it was not too messy."

Jay was sullen, "Ouch."

"He would have killed, so I killed him instead. I don't feel bad for it. When I completed that job I left the country and two days later had three-million-dollars deposited in my account. I haven't talked to the general since, but that was my one job in North Korea. I see him occasionally on TV. He is in the Supreme People's Assembly in some role, but I don't keep up with him much. I didn't reach out to him with this as I am sure he would have no allegiance," Michael continued.

Jay stayed sullen, "Like I said, you have had an interesting life."

Michael smiled, "You said that?"

Jay laughed, "Sure did."

Michael frowned, "Who, how and why?"

"Well," Jay said, "I think we know the why. The why is to get you out of hiding and into something. Right?"

"Okay," Michael said, "I will bite. What will that get anyone? Virtually no one knows who I am or my involvement with anything. I worked through a company, did what I needed and rarely met anyone involved. Most of my work was long distance and when I had to be up close or making an "accident" I left no witnesses. So who would know of me?"

Jay was direct. "Well, a few governments, including this one. You worked for them several times, taking out people they couldn't."

"Yeah, so?" Michael said.

"So someone there may have a grudge?" Jay said quickly.

"Maybe," Michael said. "Maybe it is time to call in a favor that is owed me and see what I can find out."

"Good idea," Jay said. "Really good idea. You know there is one other person who knows you with the government here."

"Yeah," Michael said, "but we will leave him alone now, won't we?"

The "Happy Scotsman" crossed over the edge of the mountains and headed towards Texas.

Chapter 50 – Degradation

"I have good news and bad news," Terry Drake said, as he walked into the cabin of the Gulfstream.

Alex looked up, "Okay, good news, please."

"We have a fix on them," Terry continued. "Their transponder just showed back up and they have a new flight plan filed."

Alex was glad he didn't have to report another failure to the general, but asked the important question, "So where to and how far away are we?"

"That's the bad news," Terry admitted. "We were heading west still and as such we are about 2,000 miles out of position. We will have to find a stop for fuel before we can get to their destination, which will work, but we need to be quick."

"...and their destination?" Alex asked.

"Filed as San Antonio, Texas. This changes things a little," Terry said dryly.

"It gives us an advantage," Alex said while turning to Barbara. "Get on the radio and listen in, see if we can pick up any chatter from them."

Barbara snapped, "On it."

"Jim," Alex continued, "we missed something. Find out why he is heading to San Antonio. There is something in the works. Something with our encounter, with the girl, with someone, that made him change directions. Find it. It has to be there. Rachel, help Jim."

Ronnie stood up. "What should I do, Master Sergeant?"

"Ronnie," Alex continued, "you get on the horn and get us a location in San Antonio we can work from. Base, hotel, building, parking lot, somewhere. And get us transport. We will need at least two vehicles, something not too flashy. Steer away from the damn black Suburbans.

They scream government. Maybe a car and a panel van. I don't care."

"No minivans," Jim looked up and said.

"Nothing in red," Rachel said to the side.

Alex glared at them.

"Master Sergeant, how should I pay for this?" Comer asked.

"I will help with that," Barbara piped in. "We can cover it with a global PO or credit card. No issues."

Cortez, who was usually quiet piped up, said, "I have arranged our new destination. It looks like we may need to stop and it will be close if we don't, maybe too close. We can probably pick up more speed if we stop and burn more fuel on speed than if we slow down and nurse it out if we can get an airport that is not backed up.

"You guys figure that out," Alex said. "I will try to get us taken care of on the ground."

"Roger," Cortez said, and she went back to flying.

The group hurried themselves to intercept the far away plane.

Chapter 51 – Realization

Madison woke up with a fuzzy blanket over her on the couch. The room glowed with a light reddish hue and she slowly stretched and looked peacefully out the massive windows over the mountains as colors danced across the skyline of early twilight.

The smells then wafted into her mind as she smelled food, the wonderful aroma of spices and combinations of vegetables and meat that made her stomach growl and suddenly ache with a need to eat.

It was at that point that the wonderfulness of memory kicked in and Madison sat up and screamed with the realization of what she had just experienced.

Abby was in the room in a moment and sat next to her. "Madison, it's okay. You were just asleep."

"But we were…". Madison began.

"Yes," Abby said calmly in a slow soothing voice. "It wasn't a good time, but you are safe now. We are back home, safe, sound and no one is coming to get you."

Madison started bawling, not crying, but truly bawling like a child does after that long pause of silence before the storm. "I have messed my life up so much," Madison began. "You were right. I should just leave and be gone forever."

"Shh, shh, shh," Abby said. "We will worry about that later. I got a message from Michael and everything is okay and will continue to be."

"Really," Madison sniffled as she calmed a little. "What did it say?"

"Well, it said 324, but for Michael it simply means, "All is well," and that lets me know he knows something and is going to deal with it."

Abby jumped up. "Anyway, the door is locked, the night is coming, we are safe and sound in the house and Janet and I have put dinner together."

Madison dried her eyes. "Do you really think we are safe?"

Abby laughed. "I know we are safe. Now go clean up and let's watch the mountains and talk for a while."

Madison got up and went down the hall while Abby went back into the kitchen with Janet.

Janet smiled. "Is she okay?"

"Sure," Abby said. "She is just not used to all of this and I am not sure if she ever could be."

Janet laughed. "It is amazing what you can get used to, isn't it?"

Abby smiled thoughtfully, "It sure is Janet, it sure is."

They had stopped at the grocery store and Janet had stayed with Madison in the Suburban while Abby got essentials so they would have some fresh meat and vegetables. She knew the lower part of the house would be full of rations and long-term food that would have worked, but it would also have tasted like rations and long-term food. Janet, in her wonderful way, had put together a great meal of pasta with chicken and a braised asparagus that smelled delicious.

"This looks amazing," Abby said.

"I don't get much time to cook on the plane, so this is wonderful. Before Jay, I used to spend a lot of time cooking for my kids, but when they grew up and left, well, I really had no one to cook for so I got out of practice," Janet replied.

"I doubt that," Abby said. "Michael and I cook almost every night. Occasionally we go somewhere, but you can imagine there are very few places you can go close to our homes."

"Bad for you anyway," Janet laughed. "Jay eats way too many

hamburgers and I need to get him off of that, though he does walk more now and is losing weight."

"If he loses too much he might be the "Happy Skinny Scotsman", Abby laughed.

"Absolutely." Janet giggled.

Janet finished the plates and Abby helped take them to the table. She went to the side of the room and looked at the wines. "White or red?" she said loudly to Janet.

"You pick," Janet yelled back. "I like Riesling, but I don't pair it with food well."

Abby picked up one of her favorite Kentucky wines, a Riesling from Jean Farris Winery in central Kentucky that was always good. She opened it and took it to the table as well.

Madison walked into the room with a ponytail, a clean, red flushed face and a less sullen look.

Abby smiled as they all sat down. As she poured the wine they looked out to the mountains in the slowly dimming light and Abby saw an eagle circling slowly. She wondered how long it would take to find its prey.

Chapter 52 – Trepidation

Jay landed the plane with the smoothness of a pilot that had been landing planes for thirty years, mostly because he had been landing planes for thirty years. As the plane eased onto the runway, he felt relief as he always did. Jay knew that getting the plane in the air was always the easy part, but landing a plane was chock full of potential issues, none of which had ever or would ever affect him, simply because he was careful.

"GYZa55 Heavy, this is SAT ground control taxi to hangar 15 on Runway 5," came a voice.

"Roger," came Jay's reply.

Michael unbuckled his seatbelts and headed downstairs to unhitch the truck as they would soon be mobile on the ground and heading to a hotel to take a break before walking into the fire. The plane continued to taxi as Michael stowed the harness and chains that had kept the Suburban from moving during the heavy g-force takeoff and landing. After checking the back of the truck, he went to the false compartments in the walls and retrieved his weapons, placing them in the back of the Suburban.

Michael felt the plane slow to a stop for a moment and then turn on its front wheel as it moved down another roadway. He finished and closed up the truck. then went back up to the cockpit with Jay.

"How are we doing?" he asked Jay.

"Almost at the hangar," Jay stated, paying attention to the road in front of him.

Michael looked up at the sky for a moment. "I would have preferred a cloudy night instead of the full moon."

"Well, Mr. Grumpy, I like the moon!" Jay laughed.

Michael was serious. "Someone is behind us, so I would rather fade into the crowd than end up in a spotlight a giant brick in the sky. It's not like everyone in the airport hasn't seen the "Happy Scotsman" and our pursuer will be able to find our plane easily."

"Would you lay off the plane?" Jay said. "You will hurt her feelings."

Michael didn't smile. "Understood. How long until we park?"

"About right now," Jay said as he geared down the engines.

Michael looked out the front and sides looking for anyone who may be approaching the plane and anything else that would be out of place. He saw nothing, but he continued to pay attention as the fuel and maintenance truck approached.

"I will be ready in a moment, Jay said as he unstrapped and began walking down to the cargo area.

Spotlights gleamed from the back and wings, lighting up the entire area around the "Happy Scotsman". The huge back door opened and Jay walked down the ramp to meet the fuel truck as Michael began backing the Suburban down the Treadway. At the last moment, Jay stepped off to the side and Michael swiftly brought the truck down to the ground, swinging it around facing it towards the rear gates.

He left the truck idling as Jay walked up to the crew and began talking to them about fueling. The men were dressed in nearly new looking, bright blue coveralls, which had Michael paying closer attention The one talking to Jay was tall and a little heavy in the middle, while his companion was a young man with tightly cut red hair.

Michael looked at the gate which looked closed and surveyed the situation. Suspicions were a part of everything Michael did at the moment as he knew he was under heavy scrutiny from unknown people. He watched closely and pulled out his FN Five-seven pistol and set it on the console of the big truck.

A truck started driving up to the other side and Michael could see it had two people in the cab; one was a woman who seemed tall from his vantage point and the second he recognized immediately from just two days ago at the base of his house. He rolled down his window.

"Jay, time to go," he yelled.

Jay turned and started running towards the truck, but the bigger man grabbed him easily. As Jay spun, the young man grabbed Jay's other arm. He quickly realized it wasn't as soft as he had guessed, when he was lifted off the ground and thrown to the side, while Jay tried to land a punch on the larger man. The larger man backed off for a moment as Jay yelled, "Get out of here."

Michael slammed on the accelerator and rocketed forward towards the gate as the truck tried to pull in front of him. He slammed on his brakes and opened the window. His FN Five-seven was in his hand in a second and he fired three times, blowing out the two front tires and splitting the radiator. He looked at Alex and as he did, nodded, then slammed on the accelerator pushing him to the gate.

Rachel jumped out of the truck and drew a 9mm, which she shot several times into the Suburban's tires. She was shocked to see they had no effect. She shot three more times into the gas tank area of the big vehicle and watched the bullets careen off the side as if they were BB's on a battleship.

The gate was locked, but it didn't stop the reinforced truck as it crushed through the chain holding it closed and ran out to the side street in front of the airport.

Alex walked back to Jim and Ronnie where they stood at either side of a now complacent Jay. Alex looked at Jay. "Where is he headed?"

"Nowhere you will find him," Jay said.

"You know we are on his side," Alex said.

"I am not sure you could understand his side and if you think you can get anything out of me, it will take too long for you to do it. By then he will be wherever he needs to be," Jay stated emotionlessly.

Rachel moved forward. "Let me get it out of him."

"Welcome to try, little girl, but I have wife and she would be pissed if I whipped a woman," Jay said in a matter of fact tone. "And for that matter, if he had not stopped engaging, he probably could have whipped you all. Be happy your little asses didn't get him pinned down."

"I have experienced that first hand," Alex said.

"From Kentucky?" Jay asked.

"Yep, just two days ago," Alex looked Jay in the eye. "Then I watched my men get killed after Michael let us go."

"It would be interesting if Michael knew that, He really dislikes someone else interfering with people he has let go, or vice versa," Jay said.

"Where is he going?" Alex asked.

"It is not my place to tell you," Jay said. "And you should feel sorry for whoever is at the other end of this. Michael has never failed."

"Once," Alex said.

Jay raised an eyebrow. "You really think he failed that time?"

"Yes, I do," Alex said.

"Then you don't know who you are chasing," Jay said dryly, "and you may never know him until you can see past that."

Alex considered for a moment, as Jay just looked at the crushed gate in front of them.

"Take him to the hangar and move his plane in as well," Alex said. "We need to sort this out and get wherever Michael is going before he goes too far."

Chapter 53 – Bastardization

Michael made his way through San Antonio quickly and efficiently, following traffic laws and making sure he wasn't followed. He knew that Alex was somewhere behind him and was curious to understand why he was still following. Michael considered the "why" for a moment. He wondered what would have made him a primary target since he had given them the North Koreans and had given no indication he was helping Madison. It was obvious there was more going on than he knew. Michael turned a corner and scanned the streets until he found a convenience store. When he did, he pulled into the partially lit lot.

He looked at the store for a moment, reached into the console and pulled out a baseball cap. Putting it on, he walked into the store, glanced around, walked to the back coolers and began looking. As he did, he glanced to each side with his peripheral vision while leering up and down as though he were deciding among the massive selection of energy drinks and plethora of plentiful "pops" the coolers held.

Michael noted there were three cameras in the store, but only the one at the register appeared real. Another one was actually unplugged and obviously non-functional. Michael almost smiled, but walked to the front of the store and looked at the smaller spinner rack of disposable cell phones.

He picked up two small cell phones and walked to the clerk, handing them to the older man behind the counter. The man was more than pleasant, with a ponytail that seemed almost like a statement for days gone by. The man fumbled a little and rang the two phones up slowly, scanning them to activate them.

"Anything else, son?" the man asked.

"No sir, that will be all."

"$44.50," the man said. "Do you want a bag with that?"

"Yes, sir," Michael said, as he gave the man forty-five dollars.

"Fifty cents is your change." the old man said, to which Michael waved it off and said, "Just drop it in the bucket." He nodded to a little bucket with a taped picture of a child on it.

"Damn shame about him, ain't it?" the old man said.

"Yep," Michael said, "I hope they find him."

"Me too," the old man said. "I hope they find him safe and sound."

"Yep," Michael said, as he walked out the door and got into the Suburban.

Looking around, Michael scanned to be sure there was no one following him or glancing in his direction. He opened both packages, assembled the phones and put the garbage from both in the bag the man had given him.

He turned on the first phone and realized it had been years since he had dialed the number he was about to call. He wasn't apprehensive, nor was he excited, scared or any other emotion. He was simply Michael and he was in his element now.

He dialed a number on the phone and waited. No voice answered, but Michael merely said, "Bastard Son".

There was a pause on the phone, "Rerouting," came a female voice.

"Well lookie fucking here who is calling home to daddy," a voice came. "You are in a world of shit boy."

"A shit I didn't create," Michael replied. "Who do you think you are sending your squads down on me? Do I have to humiliate them again?"

"You know who the fuck I am and I can do whatever the fuck I need to do to keep this country safe. But, in the spirit of things you have done for this country, I think it might surprise you to know I didn't send my men after you."

"Sure. I hogtied four yesterday and see they are here with me now," Michael said.

"Where might that be boy?" the voice came.

"You know where we are. Now tell them to back off, as I can't guarantee they won't be eliminated as well," Michael said.

"Like the others who died in Kentucky?" the voice returned.

"No American lives were lost in Kentucky," Michael said emotionlessly.

"Ah yes, you didn't know those little fuckers you caught died after they left you. Why don't you come in and we can talk about it?" the voice said.

"Not going to happen," Michael said. "Look Tarkington, you need to have them back off or it won't work in your favor."

"Now listen, you little shit," the general said, "there are things going on here you don't know about and your ass can be pegged for all of them. Turn your fucking ass in and we will handle the stupid twit's mom in Korea."

Michael paused for a second, more for effect than anything else. "I don't trust you. Never have, but you paid well," Michael said. "I called to have you back off. If you won't, you will be responsible for the consequences."

Michael hung up the phone and pulled the battery out.

He then picked up the other phone, turned it on and dialed another number.

"Hello," came the voice.

"Hey," Michael said, "I love you."

"Wow," Abby said, "I love you, too."

"Home soon, gotta go," Michael said.

"Bye," Abby returned as the phone clicked off.

Michael turned this phone off, but didn't remove the battery, then checked his surroundings again and drove down the street towards his destination.

Chapter 54 – Reaction

Abby held the phone tight to her chest and smiled and cried at the same time.

"What's wrong?" Madison said.

"It was Michael," Abby said. "He is fine."

"So why are you crying?" Madison asked.

"Something is wrong," Abby returned. "Michael said he loved me. In the past he has always said 143 before he took a job, but this time he was sure to say he loved me. I think he is worried about what is going to happen."

"Maybe he just loves you?" Janet countered.

"Maybe," Abby said, "but I know Michael and this was just not normal."

Madison smiled with a partially reassuring look. "Yeah, he is just wanting you to know he loves you."

Abby stood up and walked to the massive picture windows and looked out into the night. She could no longer see the eagle, but she knew it was there.

Chapter 55 – Fruition

"Put that little Scottish shit on the phone," Tarkington screamed in Alex's ear.

Alex pulled the phone away from his head as the volume of the voice increased. He looked across the table at Jay, who sat in handcuffs with his hands in his lap.

The room was small and probably was a hangar office at one time. Now it served as a makeshift interrogation room where Alex and Jay had been sitting for thirty minutes, getting nowhere. Neither logic nor threats had any effect on Jay, who just smiled and told Alex over and over, "It would be easier if you tried to beat it out of me."

Alex reached across the table and handed Jay the handcuff keys, then laid the phone on the table in speaker mode.

Jay lifted his hands up and set the handcuffs on top of the keys Alex had just set down, then picked up the phone.

"Are you there, you little shit?" Tarkington said loudly.

"Sam…," Jay drawled out.

"Don't give me that shit…," Tarkington started.

"Oh, Sam," Jay interrupted, "I'm a private citizen now. I'm allowed to fly anywhere I want. Now why would you pick on little old me?"

"Shut the fuck up, you overgrown skirt," Tarkington broke back in. "You need to tell us where he is going. He is walking into some serious shit alone and I don't give a fuck if he dies, but I don't need any more collateral."

"How's the daughter, Sam?" Jay said.

There was silence on the other end of the line.

"Didn't catch that, Sam," Jay ribbed in a higher pitched voice for effect.

"Is she still safe now and still happy with you knowing you kept her safe?"

"You little son of a bitch," Tarkington yelled. "Just because he did a few jobs for me, doesn't mean he gets a pass forever."

"Okay," Jay said, "I'll let your daughter know."

"You will shut the fuck up about my daughter," Tarkington said.

Alex sat and listened while Jay smiled and took another jab.

"First you send men after him and then you try to get me to talk about him. This, after all he has done for you," Jay began.

"You fucking dumbass," Tarkington said. "It wasn't me, not us and this little fuck with you didn't even know who he was reporting to at the time, so don't lay it on my old ass."

Jay raised an eyebrow, "So who did then?"

"Ask the little fuck that is there with you." Tarkington started. "Do you seriously think I haven't known where he was for years? You must be a dumb shit. I could have had him killed, but it didn't fucking matter. Get this through your little drunken ass head, there is something else going on."

Jay smiled. "I am sure it will be taken care of shortly, don't you think?"

"Sure, it may," Tarkington was calmer, "but you and I both know if he gets cornered, the collateral could be bad. By the way, you know if he kills whoever it is, I am sure we will never know why."

"Don't you mean 'fucking why'?" Jay laughed.

There was a pause for a moment, then a huge bellowing laugh.

"Damn right," Tarkington said. "Now help us get the truth."

"Let me ask you, Sam," Jay stated dryly, "if you were sitting in my chair right now and I asked you to betray Michael, would you? Right or wrong, positive or negative, to save him or not, would you tell someone enough to stop him from what he is focused on and maybe cross the 'truth/lie' line with him?"

Another pause on the phone, then Tarkington simply said, "I suppose not. I suppose not."

"Exactly," Jay said, and hit the end call button on the phone.

Chapter 56 – Triangulation

Michael drove past the supposedly abandoned building. He didn't speed up. Or slow down. He just drove. In his peripheral vision he checked out the building and turned, drove a short while and found a place to park. The darkness was soothing as he knew the element well, like a fox knows its den.

He turned off the interior lights of the Suburban, but knew it didn't matter much as the windows were dark and the lights low anyway. Taking off his seatbelt, he lowered the seat all the way back, then climbed into the back seat. From there he had access to his gear and one of his packed items was a night scope. He took it out and checked the batteries and functionality.

Michael was about 300 yards away from the building up the street with a mostly unobscured view of the front. He looked through the back window and focused on the building. It was a simple three-story structure. It had a basement with two stories above it, the basement being partially above ground. Although it was boarded up, the windows had been closed and there were cameras on the two corners he could see; very nice cameras. Michael could tell they were infrared as well and most likely, they could see him from there.

Michael looked around and scanned the area. He noticed a few homeless people on benches, as well as one staggering drunk man. The odd part was the staggering drunk man was in a trench coat. Michael knew this was trouble and decided to move to another vantage point even though Alex was somewhere in the city looking for him.

Michael eased back into the front seat and moved the seat up ready to drive. He started the car as the "drunk man" quickly stood erect and swinging open his coat, revealed a 50 caliber Michael thought was a British semi-automatic. The "drunk" swung it around and shot the front tire of the Suburban which exploded under the force of the weapon, which was an order of magnitude larger than the earlier 9mm shells that had bounced off his self-sealing tires. Michael hit the gas on the truck, but it lurched forward only to fall on the wheel and scrape noisily. It was not going anywhere; the force had made a mess of the front. A second shot rang and blew the back tire as Michael noted the homeless men getting up as well and heading towards him.

Michael reached into the console and grabbed the FN Five-seven he had stowed there. As the "drunk" aimed at the driver's side of the truck, Michael slammed open the door and opened fire. At twenty yards, Michael put five shots directly into the man's chest. Seeing him stagger backwards, Michael knew he was wearing body armor and though the FN Five-seven would most likely penetrate with some shots, it was not likely to be as lethal. With that understanding, Michael quickly shot twice into the man's head. There was no armor there and he went down immediately, the large gun clattering to the street.

The other two "homeless men", seeing their prey wasn't going to be an easy kill, slowly stalked towards him behind cars and anything else on the street or to the side they could hide behind. Michael saw them, but knew the firefight would bring more combatants quickly. He moved down the driver's side of the crippled Suburban and looked around the back. He opened the driver's side back door and reached in, grabbing out the P90. He didn't have time to get extra magazines from the back, so it would have to do.

The two "homeless men" were within thirty-feet now and Michael took slow aim on the closest. He was behind a newspaper stand and Michael fired two shots at it. He heard a "shit" from behind the stand and knew one had penetrated and he had gotten lucky, but the shot had not been fatal or incapacitating. Swinging around, he came up to the front of the car and swung over it wildly. The P90 was set to tri-burst and he shot three to each man's location as he came forward. The men, not expecting a charge, moved back for a moment, which was all Michael needed to shoot both of them with the FN Five-seven he held in his other hand. He didn't make his previous mistake and shot both of them dead center in the head.

No one else was in sight, so Michael quickly checked the bodies of the two closest men and took their weapons and all the ammo they had. He didn't know what he was up against, so being without could be a bad thing. The two M16's were army issue and the two men could have been Korean, but it was hard to tell.

Michael put their weapons in the back, checked his surroundings and went to the third man. The "drunk" was now an eyeless "drunk" as Michael's shots had pierced both eyes perfectly, right where he had aimed. His weapon lay at his side and Michael took it, along with the headset the man wore, and ran back to the car. Checking the headset, he found he had damaged it in his haste to eliminate the man. There would be no listening in to his opponents.

Michael reached into the back of the truck and pulled out his Barrett, setting it to the side of the truck. He then grabbed two mags for his P90 and two for his FN Five-seven and, slinging the Barrett onto his back, ran to a nearby building to get perspective. He usually did things from a distance and wasn't as enamored by close quarters as there were more possibilities of getting ambushed or not controlling the situation. Michael felt he should have seen the men earlier and just kept driving, but blamed the earlier confusion and interaction with Tarkington for making him less observant.

Michael made a mental note and moved into the shadows, looking for a way to get to the hospital without being spotted.

Chapter 57 – Damnation

"Master Sergeant, we may have a break on where he was going. Ronnie said if it was him he would be hiding somewhere no one would think, so I started looking at abandoned buildings and cross-checking them with the power grid. I found an old hospital just outside of town that is sucking a lot of power, but is supposed to be empty. It also is an accounting nightmare as I can't seem to find out how it is getting billed," Barbara said.

Alex said, "Show me," as he walked over to Barbara.

Barbara spun her computer around and the two of them looked at photos of the location. The boarded-up building was secluded and accessible in a warehouse district.

"I bet that's it," Alex said. "Rachel, get the group together and let's go."

Jay looked at Alex, "Well, are you leaving me here or am I going?"

Jim stopped for a moment and looked at Alex. "Might as well. Who knows how this will go and we may need operational intelligence. Hell, we might need another gun or ten."

Alex looked at Jay, "Can I trust you?"

Jay laughed, "Well, more than you can the dimwits in the building."

Jim laughed hard, "See, he is in."

Rachel walked in the room. "Rather have him with us. He makes a bigger target than me."

Jim laughed again. "Everyone but Ronnie and Alex are bigger targets than you."

Ronnie piped up, "Master Sergeant, do you want weapons hot?"

Alex looked at Ronnie. "We are not using harsh language and you better be hot and ready when we get there. Much as I hate to say it, Jim's driving second and I will drive the front. You get to ride with Jim, Ronnie."

Rachel smiled. "I will go with you rather than ride with Speed Racer here."

Jim laughed. "No respect."

The group headed into the hangar towards the two waiting vehicles, a pair of Black Audi A8's.

"Rachel and I will be in the first car. Jim, I will take lead, you will not outrun or outdrive me," Alex said.

Jim smiled. "Should I put one hand behind my back."

"Serious, now," Alex said in a stern voice.

"Gotcha," said Jim. "Will do," he said with a more serious tone.

Alex yelled to Barbara, Terry and Lisa. "Be ready if we need you."

Chapter 58 – Illumination

Michael slid into a small alleyway and checked his weapons. He had two full P90 magazines, giving him 100 rounds and what was in his partially loaded weapon. He had two full FN Five-seven mags, giving him about forty shots, plus what was in his loaded weapon as well. He checked his 50 caliber and had six shots, plus the six he carried. They were for long distance, but he didn't know what he was walking into yet.

He checked a small bag on his Barrett and it had twelve Hibben throwing knives. The knives were small, but razor sharp and up close were silent and deadly accurate. He also had a tanto survival knife which he slid onto his belt. A few other items were in the bag and he stuck them in his lower pant pocket and discarded the bag.

Michael then checked his surroundings again. Nothing close, no cameras, the alley was clear, but he knew someone would be coming soon. It was far too noisy for people to just ignore and whoever was in there was fully armed and ready for him.

Michael sprinted down the alley and to the street edge where he stopped and looked for anything of concern. The opposite street he had come to was clear and didn't have a direct view of the "abandoned" building. The street was lined on both sides with warehouses that could either be empty or full of an army waiting to take Michael down. He checked the door next to him and it opened, so he went in. As his eyes adjusted, he saw a rodent's dream home, full of pallets, dust, and little else. Not one to take chances, Michael stayed close to the pallets and walked like a hunting panther. There was no sound.

Michael guessed he was about 200 yards away from the building and the inside of this warehouse stretched about 150 yards. He closed his eyes and remembered the drive and in doing so, remembered the warehouse location on the road. It would be one street away from his target.

Michael crouched for a second and considered his options. Whoever was in that building was aware of him, so stealth would not buy him much. He had limited ammunition and could pick up weapons on the way, but would need to assault an unknown force to do so. This wasn't good, nor were the odds good.

A small sound made Michael turn. He looked through the pallets he was standing near and saw two men with M16's slowly walking through the warehouse, scanning the area. They were dressed in tactical gear and Michael had to assume they too were in body armor and probably not alone. He noticed their night vision goggles on as well and frowned for a moment. He needed to get them out of his ever growing, more complex equation quickly and efficiently. For now, Michael was hidden, but he knew it would not be long before he would stand out like a sore thumb.

Michael reached into his pocket, pulled out a small magnesium flare and attached it to his Endure survival pen that was on his hip pocket. He looked towards the men and looked for something to throw. He reached into his pocket and looked for change, then remembered giving it to the man in the convenience store. He would be stuck because he gave to a lost child. Rotten luck. On the floor he saw a glint, so he reached down and picked up a push out from an outlet. Smiling, Michael threw the coin shaped plug to his left and waited for it to hit. As it did, both men swung in that direction as he fired the mini flare towards them. The resulting light lit the room like a spotlight on steroids and actually caused the men pain as they ripped off their night gear.

That was all the time Michael needed as he stepped up and aimed the P90, shooting both men in the head. They fell quickly and Michael cautiously ran to the first man and grabbed one of the M16s and the three magazines he was carrying. He then went to the other man and took his magazines as well. Picking up the remaining weapon, he struck the barrel hard on the ground several times as quietly as he could to dent it, but doubted he achieved his goal. He wished he could jam the barrel and leave it. It was a good trick to let someone misfire their own weapon, but he didn't have the time to make sure it worked. As he laid the weapon on the ground, he continued through the warehouse towards the far side.

Michael stopped again and listened. Silence again, he was hopeful there were no additional men in this building, but he couldn't take a chance. He moved through another forty feet and stopped.

Still silence inside, but he heard a noise outside. Michael stopped and listened very carefully and watched the ground for any openings. He heard a footstep again. Rather than fire blindly, Michael held his ground and waited for the footsteps to fade. When he could hear no more he moved forward until he was less than thirty feet from his goal; the end wall.

Michael stopped, listened and all was quiet again, that was, of course until he heard and saw the "flashbang" scurry across the floor.

Michael dove across the door and covered his ears, then felt the grenade go off. The impact staggered him, but he wasn't as disoriented as he would have been had he not seen the grenade coming.

Michael rolled and pushed against a row of pallets in order to get his bearings and check his surroundings.

He saw the men coming and reached into his pocket, pulling out two Hibben throwers. He moved up to a crouch as they slowly worked their way towards him. As one man turned to scan the right, Michael stood and threw the blade. It landed square in the man's neck and he grabbed it, but fell to the ground, causing the second man to spin around. As he did, Michael threw the second knife, which caught the man in the shoulder as he ducked.

The second man dropped down for a moment and sprayed the area with M16 rounds as he crouched. Michael ducked backwards and heard the bullets careen off of nearby pallets and boxes.

"Too close," Michael thought to himself and looked back towards the man as he pulled the knife out of his shoulder.

"Best you got, boy?" the man said throwing the knife to the ground.

Michael pulled his FN Five-seven from its holster and came around the corner shooting. He had fifteen shots left in the magazine and five of them went straight into the man's head.

"Nope," Michael said, as he stooped and picked up his knife and wiped it clean on the man's shirt.

Michael quickly worked his way to the wall and moved to the corner of the building where he could get a line on the abandoned hospital.

Listening, he felt the quiet close in on him and took a moment to catch his breath.

Chapter 59 – Competition

The lead Audi came around the corner at near forty miles an hour and didn't fishtail. The smooth traction control computer and advanced systems in the car were strained as Alex pushed the car to its limits.

"Yeehaw," Jim yelled, as Ronnie held on tightly to the armrest. "About time that Alex cut loose."

"I take it back," Rachel said holding onto her weapon and her door. "I might want to be in the other car."

"Shut up and watch the GPS," Alex said simply. "How long?"

"Five minutes," Rachel said, as they tore around another corner.

Alex slowed immediately and started driving normally as houses gave way to a series of massive warehouses. Minutes passed and the warehouses seemed to go on forever.

Alex spoke into his headset, "Jim, you back there?"

"Damn, Mario, I sure am," Jim laughed.

"Mario the video game?" Ronnie said.

"Mario the race car driver." Jim said.

"Listen up, clear the chatter. We are less than five minutes from where things might go down. You need to get serious, fast," Alex stated in a harsh monotone.

"Ready," Jim said.

"Ready," Ronnie said.

"Ready," Rachel said.

"Ready?" Jay said. "Yeah, ready."

"You best be or you can stay in the car." Alex said.

The Audi's turned a corner and Alex clicked his mic. "We have smoke up ahead; slow down and be cautious."

"Roger," Jim said.

The cars drove up a few more blocks and the smoke was becoming more and more evident. In this district in the early morning darkness, it was doubtful the smoke would be noticed as much as in the light of day. They were four blocks away when Alex pulled the car over.

Alex got out and eased to the back of the car, taking in the situation as Rachel got out of the other side and walked back with him. Moments later Jim, Ronnie and Jay joined them.

"Jay," Alex started, "I am not going to regret bringing you, am I?"

"I think I have been doing this longer than you. I can follow orders. After all, I follow Michael's and I am his senior, too. You want me to follow; I will do it until you blow it. You want my respect, keep Michael and this group alive," Jay said in the first serious tone Alex had heard from him.

"I can deal with that," Alex said. Alex looked at the small team. "Rachel, Ronnie, night vision up. Jay, Jim and I will not use night vision. You are our eyes on the edges. We will keep you safe in case of light or flash fire."

The group heard gunfire echo from the area where the smoke was rising.

"223, probably an M16," Jay said.

A rapid succession of additional gunfire came right after. "Pistol, probably 5.7 x 28, which would make it Michael or someone out of a Clive Cussler book."

"Two by two by one. I will take point with Rachel as my eyes. Jim and Ronnie cover, Jay take the rear. Pay attention and Jay, watch our ass good. We got taken by Michael from there," Alex said.

"Yeah, he likes taking people in the ass," Jay laughed. Everyone smiled for a moment as Alex led them off at a fast pace to a battle four blocks away.

Chapter 60 – Ascension

Michael fired blindly and waited again. Each time he fired, a few shots came from the roof. The muzzle flash was enough to give Michael the bearing and he once again swung the 50 caliber off his back and aimed at the spot that was lit only a moment ago. He fired his FN Five-seven in the air once and waited. As the sniper raised to shoot again, Michael held his breath a moment, squeezed the trigger and the man went down.

Michael slid behind a series of crates and checked his ammunition. His P90 had less than twenty shots in it, his FN Five-seven had less than five and his 50 caliber was now empty. He had an M16 with nine magazines, giving him over 200 shots of 223 that he had picked up, but he had not used it yet.

He took a moment and unloaded the magazine from the P90 and moved the shells to his FN Five-seven and carefully discarded the P90. He covered it and noted the location so he could retrieve it later. He also set his Barrett in the same spot so it too might be retrieved. He then holstered his pistol and moved forward with the M16.

Looking to the roof, he aimed the M16 at the camera looking at him and fired once, destroying it. He switched to the second camera, fired once and missed. Someone close would have seen the irritation Michael was feeling. He never missed, ever. He took aim once more and the second camera was effectively destroyed as well.

Michael checked the weapon and was frustrated knowing it was not one of his that was meticulously taken care of, oiled, cleaned and re-sighted consistently.

He moved and waited only a moment, then walked quickly across the street to the building. There was no use being stealthy now. Most of the world probably knew he was on his way into the building, so he went to the door, slid to the side and pushed it and pulled back quickly in case it was rigged or another trap was behind it.

Nothing.

Michael moved in slowly. As he did, the darkness closed in on him and he wished he still had his night scope. Sliding over to the side of the main hall, he waited to ensure his eyes had adjusted completely.

The front door closed beside him and Michael lost a little more light. He thought for a moment and was sure it was about 5:30 in the morning by now. This could give him some light very quickly, even though the windows were boarded.

Michael could not wait it out, but walking into a snake's den would most likely get you bit, or so Rudyard Kipling had promised. Michael considered his direction and decided "up" was going to allow him to cover more than "down". He moved to the stairs at the back of the long hall and started working his way slowly up them, turning often to check behind him as he ascended.

Chapter 61 – Contradiction

Alex and his team were cautious as they approached the warehouses that reeked of smoke and ruin. Alex looked back at his team, raised his hand and spread his fingers, motioning for the group to spread out in the carnage. Several bodies were in the road, as well as the ruined Suburban. Jay "duck walked" to a man in a trench coat and saw the man's eyes had been shot out. Any other time he would have smiled.

"This was Michael," Jay said on the headset.

"Are you sure?" came the reply from Alex.

"Know many people who can put a shot in each eye of a person and use a 5.7 pistol or rifle?" Jay replied.

Jay spun as Ronnie came back behind him. "Shee-it," Ronnie said into the mic.

"Here too," Rachel said in her mic. "Multiple hits, one shot dead center between the eyes."

"Same," Jim said. "At least this guy is predictable."

Alex was at the truck. "It was an ambush and he came out ahead. Something to be said for that. Look at these wheels. Front one is ripped apart and flat, self-sealing and flat. It must have been a 50 cal or better to do this kind of damage."

Jay slid up beside him. "Yeah, not much could stop one of his Suburbans."

"Yeah, we know," Rachel said, as she walked up.

Jay moved to the wall of the closest warehouse and looked around. "We still need to move forward," he pointed up the street to where smoke was still billowing. "Whatever happened here, we missed it."

"Move up," Alex began, "Same formation. Keep it tight. The closer we get to whatever is going on, the more chance we will run into someone who isn't done."

"I thought this guy let you go and had compassion," Rachel said.

Jay broke in, "If he is your friend or has any trust for you, he will make your world a better place. If you cross him, he will put you in your place. Most likely that will be the ground, a nice little plot, usually about ten by ten, by eight feet down."

"A walking contradiction," Jim said.

"Exactly," Jay said, as they walked forward, "and it looks like right now he is on a mission to make something right."

The team moved slowly up the street towards the abandoned hospital and the carnage that surrounded it.

Chapter 62 – Obfuscation

Michael was at the top of the stairs at the entry to the second floor. He swung the heavy steel door open as he fell back against the wall.

Nothing.

For the most part his insertion had been too easy. Sure there were multiple mercenaries or soldiers, some American, some seemingly Korean, but if anyone knew him they would have been far more prepared.

Michael took a telescoping mirror from his pocket and folded it out to the length of its three-foot range. He peered around the corner using the mirror, then flipped so he could see both directions. The second floor was full of doors with a potential center station halfway to his right. Each door offered another chance at an ambush and Michael didn't like his odds once he was in the open hall.

Still, he had to finish this and it was obvious he was in the right place or else he had just pissed off someone really badly and would hate to have to say "Sorry."

Michael swung around the door almost crawling, the M16 in front of him. He moved forward slowly, panning from side to side. He was silent as a summer breeze and moved to the far end of the hall. Going to the first door he saw it had a small glass insert.

Michael used the mirror again to look into the room and saw nothing. He then moved across the hall just as quietly and slid the mirror up. Again, an empty room that also seemed like a tomb covered in dust and time.

Michael slid across the hall diagonally, watching the open hallway closely. Like before, he put the mirror up and this time in the center of the room was a barbed cage. It looked to be about ten feet by ten feet and in the center, lying on a futon, was a woman. The rest of the room had a few file cabinets, a desk and was cleaner than the previous two rooms.

Michael checked the hallway and slid lower to the ground, maneuvering his mirror under the door to see if there were explosives, wires or anything else keeping him from getting in.

Nothing.

Michael turned the door handle and it was unlocked. He moved into the room and worked his way to the side. He was still ten feet away from the cage and he could not tell if the person was dead or alive. Moving closer, he checked the cage for an entry point and found a small makeshift door.

After checking the door, he walked back to check outside and found the hall was still clear. Michael imagined a tumbleweed would have felt at home in the building right now. It was much different than his approach just minutes ago.

He checked the lock on the makeshift door and realized it was bound by wire, so he took out his survival knife and simply cut the wire, avoiding the lock completely.

He didn't enter the cage, but instead took a small piece of scrap from the floor and threw it at the body.

The mass of hair and clothes stirred, then turned to him and looked at him first with confusion, then slowly in recognition. "Michael?" Karen said, "Oh my God, Michael" she said with more urgency. "Michael, you have to get out of here. Michael, Seth hates you, more than anyone I have ever known. Michael, it is time for you to go. I will stall him…"

"Shhh," Michael said. "Madison found me." Michael smiled only slightly. "Come on, we are leaving."

"Michael, you don't understand," Karen began.

The gunshot startled even Michael and grazed his right arm. Reflex kicked in and Michael rolled to the side behind one of the file cabinets and for the first time in a long time was trapped in a situation he didn't control.

"Nice of you to join us," came the voice. "Time for us to finish this."

Michael looked at his surroundings and knew that one way or another, the voice was right.

Chapter 63 – Clarification

Alex and the team continued their move up the street and found the smoke billowing from a warehouse. As they checked doors they found the first two were locked, but a third was open and they moved inside. Alex held his hand up and checked his watch. It was less than an hour to sunrise. Soon the sky would begin to lighten and with it the questions would come; the police, the news and a dozen other things.

Alex pulled his phone and tied it to his headset.

The phone rang and then answered.

"Sergeant Alex Brown reporting in," Alex said.

A female voice this time stated, "Transferring"

"What the fuck?" the groggy voice came. "Do you know what time it is?"

"Yes, sir. 0420, sir. We have not slept, sir," Alex said dryly.

"How bad is it?" the general said.

"We need cleanup and containment. The corporal will send the coordinates."

"There will be a team there ASAP. I will leave within thirty minutes for the area," the general stated far more awake. "Did you fuck this up?"

"No sir," Alex stated. "We have yet to engage. We are playing catch up now."

"Well get the fuck in there and stop this mess. Keep the boy alive if you can. I have some questions for him,." the general stated as he hung up.

"Yes sir," Alex said to the dead phone.

The team moved forward and found two more bodies. As Alex and Jim were checking the headshots Jay spoke. "Movement, ahead seventy-five feet."

The team spread into the stacks of pallets.

"I have them," Rachel said quietly. "Six men policing, two additional down."

"Move up," Alex said, "tight and quiet."

The team walked slowly in loose formation to the forward area, with Jay watching their flank.

"Your move," Jim said to Alex when they were within thirty feet.

"Line up your shots, Ronnie take the first, Jim, second two, Rachel fourth, Jay fifth, I will have the sixth. Call ready."

"Ready," Jim whispered.

"Ready," Rachel whispered.

"Ready," Jay whispered.

"Ready sir," Ronnie whispered.

"Fire on any aggression," Alex whispered.

"United States Army, put your weapons down," Alex yelled.

The six men spun and the first began firing. The rapid fire bursts were aimed in their direction, but at no particular target. The effect was like a chain of dominos, the first shot and there were five single shots inserted in the flow, then another shot, then silence. Four men fell to the ground, but two only fell to their knees and started scanning the area.

Alex grimaced. "Shoot for the head."

"Last chance; weapons down or you're done," Alex yelled.

The two men scanned the area for a moment, then slowly put their weapons down.

Alex quietly came out in the open, still aiming at the two men. "Smart move boys. Knees please. Lock the ankles, hands on your head."

The men started kneeling as Rachel and Jim moved up to them. At the last minute they both jumped to the pair and grabbed for their weapons, hoping the close proximity would keep anyone from firing.

Rachel grabbed her assailant by the head and slammed him down to the ground face first, then stepped on the back of his neck. She quickly brought her sidearm to the same place and said, "That was fun wimp. Now sit still."

Simultaneously, Jim grabbed his attacker by the neck and held him over his head. The man's arms flailed for purchase, but Jim had thrown him clear over his head and then threw him down hard on his back. The man landed with an audible "oof" as Ronnie shoved his weapon into the man's face. "Thanks, kid," Jim said smiling.

Alex bent down to the man on his back, "That was stupid. We could have killed you."

Jay was next to Rachel now and rolled the first man over and found he was dead. The force of Rachel's blow had pushed his face into the ground, breaking his nose at an awkward angle, most likely sending shards of bone into his brain.

"Seems we did kill this one," Jay said.

"Answers quick," Alex said to the survivor.

The man was a seasoned mercenary or worse. He had nothing to say.

"Fine," Alex said. "We will let Tarkington deal with him."

"The general?" the man questioned.

Alex perked up. "Yep, the same. It is who I work for."

"Then we have problems, because that's who I thought I was working for," the man said.

"He is on his way here, so you have about thirty seconds to spill. Do we need to dial him in?" Alex said.

"I'll need confirmation," the man said, but Alex was already dialing the phone.

Chapter 64 – Interpretation

"Still alive Michael?" the voice came.

"With that shot?" Michael said dryly. "Of course."

Michael scanned the area and looked for alternate cover. There was little to work with, so he was tactically pinned down behind the file cabinet.

He checked his arm and it was less than a scratch. M more of the cut was probably caused by the burn of the cloth than any actual contact with a bullet. He knew he had about twenty rounds in his FN Five-seven and still had his knives.

He pulled out the telescoping mirror again and it was just he and Karen in the room. As he panned, there was a gunman at the door. The man was tall and handsome, his angular face was familiar. He shot at the mirror and missed, so Michael moved it up and down slowly. The man aimed and missed again. Upon that shot, Michael turned quickly and shot twice at the door.

"I never really expected you to make it here," the man said.

"I this and I that. Who are you?" Michael said.

"I am surprised you don't recognize me," the man said. "It took forever for me to find out who you were and longer to find out what you looked like, but the CIA is a good place for finding answers."

"Sure," Michael replied dryly, watching the man in the mirror as he tried to aim at it. Another shot echoed and again the man missed.

"So, you are CIA?" Michael asked while still moving the mirror. Another shot rang out; another miss.

The man was leaning out a little more, taking slow aim and showing part of his right side as he tried to get a bead on Michael's mirror.

Michael checked his weapon and held fast with one hand as he continued to move the mirror with the other.

"I am probably not CIA anymore," the man said. "It would have been so much easier if those twits I sent in would have killed you. When I leaked you were going to turn over evidence on North Korea, the North Koreans were predictable and sent men as well. When I eliminated all seven, you left alive. I sealed my fate as far as being part of the agency."

"All this for me?" Michael said as another shot missed. "Oh, and by the way, they don't teach you guys how to shoot a 9mm very well, do they?"

"Oh yes," the man said. "I had been looking for you for quite a while until I stumbled upon Karen. She was a dingbat that was always on the CIA radar and after taking her in, she mentioned your name and that you used to be a bad person. She wasn't smart enough to keep her mouth shut and when I learned her daughter used to date you, it all started to fit. I knew I couldn't find you, but I was hoping the threat to her mom would make her find you. Worked like a charm."

Michael watched closely and the man fired again. This time Michael swung his arm around and fired three shots into where the man's leg was a moment ago.

"Fuck," the man yelled.

Michael looked in the mirror again and no one was in the door.

He heard the man talking in the hallway. "Get your asses up here now. I don't care how many of you there are left."

Michael quickly moved to the center where Karen was crying in the cage. "Get out here, Karen."

"I have messed everything up," Karen sobbed.

"Get out here now," Michael said and grabbed her arm and yanked her out of the makeshift cell. "Now get behind the file cabinet over there and keep quiet."

Karen looked in Michael's eyes and he looked away from her. "Do it now," he said, while he watched the door.

Michael stared at the door while he listened to Karen getting behind a second file cabinet. He watched a small mirror in a hand come slowly around the door edge. With a swift movement Michael shot the mirror, blowing it up and watching blood spray from the man's hand.

"Ssssshhhhhhit!!!!!!!!" the man yelled.

"Hurts a bit," Michael said dryly.

"Fuck you," the man said and Michael saw the man's left hand awkwardly pull his gun out and fire nine shots. Then silence. Michael heard the magazine drop and sprinted to the door. He turned the corner where the man was slapping his magazine into the weapon. As the man lifted the weapon, Michael aimed and shot it out of his left hand.

"You were a bad shot before," Michael said, aiming at the man's head. "Switching to left didn't improve you."

The man grabbed his hand tightly, dancing around in pain. Below them Michael heard the sound of gunfire, then a clatter on the stairs, then more gunfire.

The sun was rising now as Michael held the gun to the man's head. "Last time," Michael said. "Who are you?"

"Go ahead," the man yelled. "Kill me like you did my father. I know my mother paid you to kill him and now she is living with some old guy in the Bahamas. My brother and I will never be the same because of her. And you."

The man had fallen to his bottom and was now sliding backwards slightly.

"You are such a coward for killing my father," the man said, "He was a great man."

"Who are you?" Michael said again loudly.

"Seth Fielding," the man spat.

Michael considered for a moment, looked at the man and lowered his gun slightly.

Michael laughed; not a little laugh but a bellowing laugh that nearly shook the room.

"So you are one of the two sons," Michael said, kneeling down with the FN Five-seven again pointed at the man's mid-section.

More gunfire rang out from below. Michael glanced away for a moment and Seth jumped at him, grabbing the pistol around the barrel.

Michael let go of the weapon and Seth fell backwards as Michael drew another Hibben and threw it into Seth's hand.

Seth screamed in pain. "Damnit, damnit, damnit!"

Michael bent down and picked up his FN Five-seven and holstered it. "All this death was for your father?"

Seth picked up the Hibben and threw it at Michael. It landed sideways across the room, not even close. Seth scurried backwards as Michael stood and walked forward towards him.

"You killed him," Seth screamed. "You killed him for my bitch of a mother."

"Seth," Michael said, "ever wonder why I disappeared? I have the date and time in my head forever. Your father paid me to kill your mother and as I watched her crying for the way she was treated, I had enough.

So I killed the man who paid me. Ruins the jobs rolling in when you go against your target."

"You lie," Seth said, still scurrying backwards.

Michael laughed again. "Why would I lie? I have won. I could kill you or let you live. All this carnage and I blew up a house, so you could hunt me down for the wrong crime. Yes, I killed your father, but not because someone paid me. I killed him because he was a selfish arrogant sexist pig that thought of women as property." Michael stood and paused for only a moment. "Just like my father. Your father paid me to kill your mother and was gloating about it as he waited for me to pull the trigger."

The footsteps were pounding up the stairs now and Michael saw Karen come around the corner. There were a lot of moving parts at this point and in moments it would all be over.

Chapter 65 – Elevation

There were six men waiting for them as they entered the building. Alex had walked in first, but had been pulled back by Rachel as she saw the men coming down the hall. Jim had pulled the doors back giving them visibility and they had worked the men down, one at a time. Their captive had given them enough intel to know there were quite a few inside and they were not all company. Although Alex announced himself, this group wasn't interested in talking and only fired. The team didn't want to kill friendlies, but the situation and timeliness made it impossible to know who was who.

Jay had proven himself to be an asset quickly as he was on the street lying on a car. As he saw men, he had convinced them to get under cover by a few shots above their heads.

The men had worked their way to the stairs which appeared to be their initial goal. Alex nodded and his team advanced. Ronnie got a little too cocky and thought he was shot in the leg. Alex checked and upon examination it was just a ricochet of concrete from a wall. Now they were in a standoff with the men on the stairs and his team hunkered down around the hall of the first floor.

The team had heard the shots from the upper level and knew there was a gunfight there as well, but didn't have the ability to move any faster than they were right now. It was six on five, and Alex felt they had the advantage.

It felt good knowing everyone was fine. Jay kept the back covered as he and Jim moved forward.

"Just like old times," Jim said.

"Funny, I didn't like the old times either," Alex said dryly.

"Sure you did, you stayed," Jim said, as he ducked behind a door. Jim's temporary shield dented four times with 223 pockmarks, but the door was made of good old-fashioned American steel and only bent, didn't give way.

"Don't make them like they used to," Jim said.

"Serious, team, we still have targets," Alex said sternly.

Jim laughed. "I think jokes gave us the advantage."

Jay laughed as well "I think you're right," he said.

"Jim, Rachel, find a back way," Alex said. "Ronnie on my six. Jay, keep our asses safe."

Without any verbal response, the team split. Jay covered from the door and kept glancing outside as the sky lit up with bright pinks and ambers. "Not much time left 'til dawn," Jay said. "I bet we got a lot of company by then."

"According to the general, we could have cleaners here any minute," Alex returned.

They heard shots down the hall.

"Alex, we are heading up the back stairs. We had a visitor, but Rachel convinced him to stand down," Jim said over the com.

"Dead?" Alex asked.

"No, but he has a big ouchy on his head," Jim said.

Alex worked his way to the edge of the stairwell going up. "United States Army, put your weapons down."

"We are the United States Army, put your weapons down," a voice returned.

"I am under the command of General Tarkington; we have already captured one of your men who has given us necessary intel. You are all being led by a traitor with a personal agenda," Alex said.

Shots were fired from halfway up the stairs again.

"Seth is a traitor with a personal agenda. Don't die for this, it is not for your country," Alex said. "I am Master Sergeant Alex Brown, in command. Last chance to put your weapons down."

Alex heard discussions, then a voice, "We are coming down."

The men walked down the steps with weapons hanging in front.

"Jay, cover," Alex said as the men hit the bottom step.

"This shit better be for real," the lead soldier said.

"You are going to be in a world of hurt boys," Alex said. "The general is on his way now."

"Ahh, shit," a man in the back said.

Alex motioned the men over and pointed to the floor as the men sat down next to the wall. Jay covered them from the door as the sky became even brighter. "Jay, stay here and cover these men. Ronnie with me."

Jay moved back and covered the men, while Alex and Ronnie moved up the stairs quickly to the first landing.

"Jim, status," Alex said.

"Back stairs," Jim said. "Almost to the floor."

"Landing in fifteen," Alex said, as he worked his way up with Ronnie at his back. In fifteen seconds they would come out on the two sides of the floor and somewhere in between was Michael and more.

Chapter 66 – Intersection

"LIAR!" Seth yelled.

"Why would I lie?" Michael said. "I have the advantage. I am in control and you have lost. It will be easier for you if I kill you, as I am sure the government will not show you much mercy."

"You lie," he said as he hung his head low. "My father loved us."

"No," Michael said, "he loved the thought of you. In the end, you have dishonored him and your mother."

Seth seemed to be crying, then seething, all in mere moments.

In a quick movement, Seth reached into his pant leg and pulled out a small revolver. In a fast fluid motion, the gun was shot out of Seth's hand by Michael.

Michael holstered his smoking weapon and shook his head. "You still don't get it, Seth. You researched me and what I have done, but it does not define who I am. Your father, my mother and my experience defined who I am as I chose a new path. You have no clue who you are, do you? I defined you and you couldn't know who I am without talking to me and understanding who I am."

"Seth," Karen said, "I was wrong. Michael is not a monster."

Michael raised an eyebrow.

"No, Karen," Michael said quietly, "I was, I am and I will be, but I control the monster, it does not control me."

Michael heard running up the steps and saw men clear the top stair as he dove to the edge of the room and drew his FN Five-seven.

"Michael," Alex yelled, "It's the good guys."

Michael peered out and assessed the situation. He knew Alex from only a day ago. He didn't know the others and turned quickly and saw two behind as well.

"That remains to be seen," Michael said dryly.

"Jay is downstairs covering the front. Who is this?" Alex said, pointing to Seth who still sat dumbfounded in the center of the hall.

"A piece of my past that should be forgotten," said Michael, "and the person who caused all of our troubles."

Alex went forward to Seth. "You killed my men?"

Seth looked up. "Just kill me, Michael." He said with a sullen look. "I'm dead already."

"No, I am sure Tarkington will want the pleasure of your company," Alex said. "He is on his way here."

"Well isn't that great," Michael said. "The Asshole Father."

Alex looked perplexed as he zip tied Seth's hands, even as Karen pleaded with him to be careful.

"...and who is this?" Alex asked.

"This is the woman whose daughter begged me to save her in North Korea. We are a bit far away from North Korea, but it was a fun ride getting here," Michael said.

"Are we done?" Alex questioned.

"When I am home, we are done," Michael said.

"Could you holster your weapon?" Alex said.

"As soon as the two behind me stand down," Michael said, and glanced back again. "I am sorry, Alex. I only know you here."

Alex motioned and Jim and Rachel put their weapons down.

Michael holstered his weapon and looked at Alex as the sun flooded the room with light. He looked to an un-boarded window, saw the sunrise and smiled.

"Good morning, Seth," Michael said, "and welcome to your own personal hell. I hope you find your way out of it."

Chapter 67 – Introspection

The hangar in the San Antonio airport was bustling with activity. The "Happy Scotsman" was refueled and ready to go, Seth was in custody and Michael retrieved his P90 and Barrett so he could take them home, clean them and make them perfect again.

Another Gulfstream pulled into the edge of the hangar and the door rapidly opened.

General Tarkington walked down the stairs and over to the small group sitting around a toolbox.

"Well, if it isn't the Bastard Son," Tarkington said, as he walked to them.

"If it isn't the Asshole Father," Michael shot back at him.

"You really are a fucking mess, aren't you Michael?" Tarkington said.

Alex, Rachel, Ronnie and Jim were a little perplexed by the interaction.

"I suppose I am, but it does not matter. Your daughter still loves me and I love her more every day," Michael said.

Realization dawned on the small group.

"So, when the fuck are you going to make her honest or at least ask the question?" Tarkington asked.

"Well before you stop cussing," Michael said.

Three men stumbled out of the plane, one in a cast, one with a broken nose.

"I suppose she is safe," Tarkington said. "I tried to get her, but between Abby and your thug, these fucking idiots couldn't get her to a safe house."

Michael laughed. "I have a safe house now and she lives in it with me."

"Until you move again," Tarkington said. "I had them hold you just so I could ask you a favor."

Michael thought about it. "Your people got me into this mess. I had to kill some people that probably didn't deserve it because of one of your company trained psychopaths, but you did clean up the mess. Sure, what's the favor?" Michael said in a semi sing-song tone.

"Tell my daughter I love her...," Tarkington said, "...and ask her to call me sometime."

Michael softened. He saw the general in a different light for a moment. "Will do, when I get there. Jay, can I get a ride?"

Jay laughed while ushering Karen and Michael over towards the "Happy Scotsman".

"Stay out of trouble, you little fucker," Tarkington yelled. "I don't want to clean up another mess."

"Then clean up your own house with good people, like Alex," Michael yelled, "and don't bother sleeping retirees."

Tarkington laughed.

While the "Happy Scotsman" was taxiing out, Tarkington talked to the small group. "You know this isn't over. There is a lot going on in the world and idiots like this fucking Seth are everywhere. I could use a good group to keep me honest. Maybe watch over people that are out there like Michael. Are you four interested?"

The group paused for a moment.

"Don't make me fucking wait on this. There are a lot of little shits like you in the world," Tarkington barked.

"I am in," Alex said.

"Me too," Rachel said happily.

"I'll do it," said Ronnie.

They all looked at Jim, who was still quiet. He looked at each of them and said, "What?" while bugging his eyes out.

"Are you in?" Alex said.

"Sure," Jim said. "I was just marveling at the general's touching moment and the fact his daughter is shacked up with a master killer."

Tarkington glared as Alex said, "He is in. Where should we report?"

Tarkington was still glaring as he said, "Get your asses to Kentucky. I will advise the rest of your group on the fucking plane while you are in the air and tell you where to be next week. For now, clean up your affairs and get ready for the ride of your life."

The small group walked to the plane as the general and his small crew walked to theirs. Only local crews remained to clean up whatever was left of the mess in San Antonio.

Epilogue

While Michael, Karen and Jay flew to Dubois, Michael called Abby and told her to meet them at the airport. He also told her how much he loved her, how he had met her dad in San Antonio and he filled her in about the whole affair, all on a secure line.

Michael arranged a flight with Jay back to Kentucky to drop Karen and Madison off and hoped it would be the last he would see of them.

As they landed, there was a happy reunion while Karen hugged Madison and Janet kissed Jay.

Michael looked at Abby. "Missed you."

"Missed you, too," Abby said. They kissed passionately for a moment, then said their goodbyes to the group. For a moment they watched the "Happy Scotsman" taxi and takeoff. Michael could only imagine the argument Jay once again had with the tower to get his plane out.

Michael hugged Abby again and held her tightly. "You know I love you?" he asked.

"Yes. You know I love you?" she said.

"I do," Michael said, as they walked to the car.

Michael and Abby held hands as they drove to the house. Michael's hands traced little circles on her wrist and he smiled as they pulled into the garage. The door to the interior of the house was cracked open.

Michael reached into the console and quickly got out his FN Five-seven and checked the slide for a round. "Did you leave the door open?" he asked.

"No," Abby said "I am sure."

"Stay here," Michael said.

"Not happening," Abby said, as she got out of her side of the car.

Michael made a symbol for quiet and they both walked into the main downstairs room together. The lights were off in the room, but Michael's computer room door was open, the lights were lower than usual, but on nonetheless. Small mini strobes seemed to come from his room, like dancing fireflies in the darkness.

Michael slipped into the room with his weapon in front of him as someone sat at his computers playing a video game with giant battleships criss-crossing his monitors.

The chair spun around and the huge man from the parking lot in Dubois smiled.

"Sorry, Michael," he said. "I was getting bored waiting. No viruses or other silliness installed, just World of Warships."

"He is the one who saved us in Dubois," Abby said, while standing slightly behind Michael.

"Why shouldn't I just kill you for breaking into my house?" Michael asked.

To Michael's right, then to his left, came two small growls. "You can kill me," the man said, "but then they would kill you. Any two of us may die, but in the end, you and Abby would be dead, too. I really don't want that; I have been watching over you for too long to see you die because of me."

"Watching over me?" Michael asked.

"Put your gun away so the dogs will calm down," the man said.

Michael put his weapon in the back of his pants and immediately the dogs quieted. Then Michael repeated, "Watching over me?"

"Since your mom died." The man stood up, stretching his massive frame then relaxing. "My name is Alan. I was an analyst and a part of a few agencies in Kentucky. Once upon a time I met your mom. She was a super woman and we talked quite a bit. I had never met anyone with such honor, devotion and passion for life and for her child." Alan walked to the dog to Michael's right as Michael turned to watch him. He crossed his arms.

Alan continued. "You see, Michael, I am patient and I watch people and listen. She was unhappy, but wanted to take care of you forever. At the same time, she felt she lost touch while you were in college and you were more than a little headstrong. I know you were going through some interesting times and your father was manipulating you. She understood you were confused by all of it."

Abby looked at Michael to see how he was taking all of this. His face belied no emotion at the moment. Abby reached up and grabbed his hand and squeezed it. He squeezed back.

Alan reached down and stroked the giant black dog while he continued. "In the end it all didn't matter. When your father killed her, I was angry and upset. I saw what happened to you and how angry you were at the trial and decided I needed to keep an eye on you. I knew what you were planning after the verdict and was worried you wouldn't be able to live with it, so I broke into your house and changed your sights the night before your father was released. After he died, I saw you had no issues, so I never tried to contact you. I am in a similar business and kept an eye on you from time to time. I mostly just help people now."

Michael shook his head. "So if you doctored my sights, how did I kill my father?" his tone indignant.

"You didn't, Michael," Alan said in a nonchalant tone as he began taking off the strange necklace over his head. Alan stood and walked up to Michael, handing him the necklace. Michael looked at the piece of metal.

"50 cal?" Michael said.

"Yours," Alan said, "removed from the wall behind where your dad was shot. The kill shot was mine. I dug this out of the wall while they were investigating. I was in the middle of it all and kept the investigation from ever getting close to you."

Michael stared at the bullet. He grabbed Abby's hand tightly with his other hand. "Why?"

"Because, Michael. No matter what your Dad did, he was still your dad and I didn't want you to live with what you were planning on doing. No matter what, I wanted to honor your mom as you should have, no matter what I had to do to make things right. In another life, your Dad would have cared for your mom and treated her right. I could never do that, so for her friendship, I honored her by choosing this path," Alan said.

"Perhaps my gift to you will give you peace." Alan stood up. "Perhaps you already had peace." Alan made a clicking sound with his mouth and the dogs stood quickly and ran out to the other room. "If you ever need me, I will be around. And next time I tell you to be wary, be wary."

Alan reached out his hand. Michael stared at the bullet for a moment, then slowly lowered Abby's hand. He reached out and shook Alan's hand.

"I don't know what to say," Michael said.

"Nothing," Alan said. "I will see you around." Alan looked at Abby. "Take care of him. He loves you and that is the most precious thing in the world."

Alan walked out the door and they heard the garage inner door close, followed by the garage door lowering.

Michael was speechless, but after a moment he looked down at Abby and peered into sparkling blue eyes. He lowered his head and kissed her with a tear in his eyes. "I love you so much," he paused, "no matter what."

"No matter what," Abby said as she pulled him down to kiss her again.

Michael and Abby will return in *Sinful Father*

Made in the USA
Columbia, SC
15 June 2018